Suddenly, out of the darkness, Noah Rider appeared.

A gasp esc̶͟͞ ͟ ͟und at the sound an̶ ̶̶̶er have expected.

He kissed

Sudden an̶ ̶̶ ̶̶̶ ̶̶̶nd not, he kissed her. She responded, unable not to, and heat rocketed through her again.

He broke the kiss, and she suddenly realized that he'd kissed her to keep her quiet, to keep her from alerting their captors.

But then he whispered, "I've been wanting to do that for days."

She wanted to say that she had, too, wanted to believe that keeping her quiet hadn't been his only reason.

But even if it hadn't, where did that leave them? Where did they go from here?

Nowhere, she realized, unless they got out of this alive. And there was a very real possibility that they wouldn't....

Dear Reader,

Once again, Intimate Moments invites you to experience the thrills and excitement of six wonderful romances, starting with Justine Davis's *Just Another Day in Paradise*. This is the first in her new miniseries, REDSTONE, INCORPORATED, and you'll be hooked from the first page to the last by this suspenseful tale of two meant-to-be lovers who have a few issues to work out on the way to a happy ending—like being taken hostage on what ought to be an island paradise.

ROMANCING THE CROWN continues with *Secret-Agent Sheik*, by Linda Winstead Jones. Hassan Kamal is one of those heroes no woman can resist—except for spirited Elena Rahman, and even she can't hold out for long. Our introduction to the LONE STAR COUNTRY CLUB winds up with Maggie Price's *Moment of Truth*. Lovers are reunited and mysteries are solved—but not all of them, so be sure to look for our upcoming anthology, *Lone Star Country Club: The Debutantes*, next month. RaeAnne Thayne completes her OUTLAW HARTES trilogy with *Cassidy Harte and the Comeback Kid*, featuring the return of the prodigal groom. Linda Castillo is back with *Just a Little Bit Dangerous*, about a romantic Rocky Mountain rescue. Finally, welcome new author Jenna Mills, whose *Smoke and Mirrors* will have you eagerly looking forward to her next book.

And, as always, be sure to come back next month for more of the best romantic reading around, right here in Intimate Moments.

Enjoy!

Leslie J. Wainger
Executive Senior Editor

Please address questions and book requests to:
Silhouette Reader Service
U.S.: 3010 Walden Ave., P.O. Box 1325, Buffalo, NY 14269
Canadian: P.O. Box 609, Fort Erie, Ont. L2A 5X3

Just Another
Day in Paradise
JUSTINE DAVIS

Silhouette®

INTIMATE MOMENTS™

Published by Silhouette Books

America's Publisher of Contemporary Romance

SILHOUETTE BOOKS

ISBN 0-373-27211-1

JUST ANOTHER DAY IN PARADISE

Copyright © 2002 by Janice Davis Smith

Visit Silhouette at www.eHarlequin.com

Printed in U.S.A.

Books by Justine Davis

JUSTINE DAVIS

lives in Kingston, Washington. Her interests outside of writing are sailing, doing needlework, horseback riding and driving her restored 1967 Corvette roadster—top down, of course.

A policewoman, Justine says that years ago, a young man she worked with encouraged her to try for a promotion to a position that was, at that time, occupied only by men. "I succeeded, became wrapped up in my new job and that man moved away, never, I thought, to be heard from again. Ten years later he appeared out of the woods of Washington State, saying he'd never forgotten me and would I please marry him. With that history, how could I write anything but romance?"

Once upon a time, there was a genre of books that was sadly misunderstood by anyone who didn't read them. Those who did read, loved them, cherished them, were changed by them. But still, these books got no respect on the outside. In fact these books were belittled, denigrated, held up as bad examples, while their readers and authors were sneered at and insulted by people who, although they never read the books, had somehow arrived at the idea that it was all right to slap others down for their choices. But those readers and authors kept on in the face of this horrible prejudice. Why? Because they found something in these books that they found nowhere else. Something precious, that spoke to them in a very deep and basic way.

Then one day, this beleaguered genre was given a gift. A fairy godmother, if you will, a person with an incredible knowledge of these books and why they worked, and an even more incredible generosity of spirit. A one-person support system who gave so much to the writers of these stories, and was ever unselfish with her time and that amazing knowledge. And her endorsement counted for something; readers took her word and knew they would rarely be disappointed. She was a rock, a pillar on which the genre depended. Her loss has left a gaping hole that can never be filled, and will always be felt by those who love these books—and loved her.

For those reasons and so many more, the Redstone, Incorporated series is dedicated to

MELINDA HELFER

Lost to us August 24, 2000, but if heaven is what it should be, she's in an endless library, with an eternity to revel in the books she loved. Happy reading, my friend....

Chapter 1

"It's scary to see that here in paradise."

Noah Rider nodded at Redstone Inc. pilot Tess Machado as they looked out the parked jet's window at the airport terminal. There was something inherently ominous about men in camouflage anywhere, but it seemed even worse in a tropical paradise. Especially when those men in camouflage had automatic rifles slung over their shoulders.

He called up a memo on his laptop computer, knowing he needed to notify the main office that things might be worse than suspected. Redstone had received reports that the rebels were calling it a political uprising, when in fact it was simply a rebellion against the suppression of the drug traffic. But if the government of Arethusa felt the need to guard the airport, it did not bode well for continued peace in this Caribbean island paradise.

"It's a good thing the resort guests coming in next week won't be making this stop," Tess said.

Rider looked at the woman who had been Joshua Redstone's personal pilot for six years, ever since the head of

Redstone Inc. had reluctantly acknowledged he had to work during a flight too often to keep doing all the flying himself.

"Yes," he agreed. "It's not the most welcoming sight for vacationers."

He knew some would arrive at the newest Redstone resort in their own planes, some via Josh's private fleet—probably even the new Redstone Hawk IV he sat in now—but none should need a refueling stop before landing at the new airstrip at Redstone Bay. They had only stopped to pick up a shipment for the resort; the Hawk IV had more than enough range to make the trip from India nonstop.

"Do you know who you're bringing in next week?" he asked her. When Tess wasn't piloting Josh, she was part of the Redstone pilot pool, at her request; she loved flying. She traveled almost as much as Noah, and he wondered what kind of strain that put on her relationship with the stockbroker she'd been seeing. It had certainly been enough to destroy his own marriage, and the one serious relationship he'd had since. He kept his mouth shut, however; Tess was like a big sister to him, and she'd made it clear if there was any advice giving to be done between them, he'd be on the receiving end.

"I'm not sure yet," she answered. "But if we have to stop for any reason, it'll be in Antigua," Tess said, pushing dark bangs back with her fingers as she looked out the window once more.

"Good idea." Her gesture made Rider think of his own appearance, and he rubbed a hand over his bewhiskered face.

As Tess returned to the cockpit he rose and walked back to the head, although it had always seemed ludicrous to him to call something as elegantly appointed as this bathroom a head. Josh had drawn the line at gold-plated fixtures for this, his own personal jet, but everything was still the highest quality. As were all the planes built by Redstone. From the smallest prop to the biggest jet they made, the fleet that was the foundation of Joshua Redstone's business empire was all pure class.

But the quality of the mirror couldn't help the reflection, Rider thought as he peered at himself. He looked like what he was, a man who'd been running too long on too little sleep. His dark hair was tousled and overdue for a haircut, he'd gone beyond fashionable stubble sometime yesterday afternoon—whatever time zone that had been in—and his eyes were as much red as blue. But nobody would really care what he looked like as long as he acknowledged the hard work they'd been doing.

As they began to roll again, loading completed, Rider went back to his seat and glanced out at the military men once more. He wondered for a fleeting moment if his clever boss had done this intentionally, so he'd get a firsthand look at the situation on Arethusa. But he discarded the thought; if that were the case, Josh would have sent Draven, or someone else on the security-and-troubleshooting staff, not him. He was strictly a detail man, and hadn't been this close to serious weaponry since the years spent hunting with his father in the wilds of Montana. He might once have been able to stalk even a wary skunk, but these days boardrooms were as close as he came to throat-slitting violence. And most times, that was close enough for him. He was glad to leave Arethusa behind.

By the time they were approaching Redstone Bay, Rider had his checklist prioritized. First the staff meeting to thank them all for what they'd done so far, then individual meetings. Then he would—

Tess's voice crackled over the intercom. "We're about to land, Mr. Rider."

Smiling at the formality she always maintained once in the cockpit, Rider pressed the intercom button on the console beside the spacious table. "Thanks."

He'd asked for a circuit of the island before they landed, so he could see what the place looked like from all approach directions. He had a knack—some called it a brain glitch—for remembering maps and plans, and he could call up the original planned layout at will. So now he studied the view below, nodding slowly.

They'd done a good job, kept the disruption of the landscape to a minimum and the buildings in keeping with the style of this part of the world. Not that there was any lack of luxury, but there was no towering concrete monolith of a hotel here—that wasn't Redstone's style. The four-story buildings were arranged around a large courtyard, and were low enough to be masked by the inevitable palm trees. A number of small, elegant and very private bungalows were scattered among the trees. The swimming pool at one edge of the courtyard was also subtle, designed to look more like a natural lagoon and grotto than something built by man.

Even the landing strip, Rider thought as they banked for the last turn, wasn't a huge scar on the land, but had been landscaped with exquisite care to maintain the most natural look possible.

He sat back in the leather seat, nodding with satisfaction. This, he thought, was going to be smooth sailing.

Paige Cooper turned a page in her leather-bound journal, ran her finger down the center to make it lie flat, and picked up her pen. Then she set it down again, caught unexpectedly by a wave of emotion. She closed the journal and gently touched the cover, tracing the intricate Celtic design on the teal-green leather. Moisture welled up behind her eyelids as she fought down a stab of fierce longing for those days past, when life had been good and her son, Kyle, had loved her enough to save all his allowance for three months to buy this for her birthday.

As if her thoughts had summoned him, she saw Kyle out of the corner of her eye, leaving his room and walking toward the front door of the bungalow they'd been given to live in while she was on the staff. She knew the instant he realized she was there by the way his normal, gangly-fifteen-year-old walk became a slow, dragging shuffle, with his shoulders slumped as if he bore the weight of an unfair world.

She smothered a sigh and tried for a cheerful tone. "Where are you off to?"

He stopped dead. Only his head turned toward her as he gave her a look of such exaggerated incredulity that she winced inwardly. Everything seemed to be over-the-top with him these days.

"Nowhere." His voice was bitter, acidly so. "Since I'm in the middle of noplace, with no friends and nothing to do, I'm going nowhere."

She reined in the urge to order him not to use that tone with her. She knew he was having a hard time just now, and tried not to focus on the superficial symptoms of that.

"It must be awful to feel that way," she said, her voice carefully even. "Especially when lots of people would love to be here."

It stopped him, but not for long. "*Those* people would be here by choice. *They* wouldn't be dragged away from home, forced to leave all their friends and even their own stuff."

She'd known when she'd taken the Redstone job last month that this could be a problem. "I told you," she said patiently, "as soon as we get a little ahead you can have Danny come for a visit."

"Danny? That little geek?" Kyle sneered.

"He's your best friend."

"Maybe when I was seven. You just don't get it, do you? I've grown up, I can't hang around with those little kids."

"He's your age," Paige pointed out.

"It isn't the age," Kyle said haughtily, "it's the maturity. Danny is still a kid. All he thinks about is school and sports and computers. He doesn't have a life."

Paige's patience ran out abruptly. She stood up, not that

it helped much now that Kyle was nearly two inches taller than her five foot four.

"You think it's more mature to have a police record that will follow you the rest of your life? That your life is best spent playing video games endlessly? That it's more grown-up to hurt the people that love you the most?"

Kyle flushed. "The one that loved me the most is *dead*," he shouted, and ran out the door.

Paige sank back into her chair, blinking rapidly. The truth boiled up inside her, and she was thankful Kyle had gone. She didn't think she could have held it back this time. But telling him would only hurt him all over again, and he'd been through enough. He'd adored his father and now he was dead, and beyond that nothing much mattered.

Except that now, at fifteen, that same loving son hated her. And never let pass a chance to tell her yet again how she had ruined his life and he would never, ever forgive her.

She fought down the urge to cry; she'd wept enough over this to know it was a useless exercise. She straightened her spine, opened the journal and picked up her pen.

Sometimes, she told herself firmly, you just have to do what you know is right, and damn the torpedoes. Or whatever that saying was.

She found her page and glanced at what she had written before: "Nothing much happens here in Redstone Bay."

It suddenly struck her this was very much like the opening of an old, much-loved book her mother had handed on to her. It had been written on a postcard in the story, but the sentiment had been the same. In the book it had also been the precursor to chaos for the unsuspecting heroine.

Paige smiled wistfully at her own whimsy. She lifted her gaze and looked around at paradise. A slight, balmy breeze rustled the palm fronds, but barely stirred the few strands of hair that had escaped her braid. She couldn't imagine a more peaceful place. The strife she'd heard the hotel staff talking about seemed distant and unreal in this haven of serenity.

And that serenity was exactly what she'd come here for. It had been difficult, giving up her home. But she'd had enough of the brutal streets of Los Angeles. And more than that, she'd had too much of what they were doing to her son. She empathized more than he would believe with his struggle to go on without his father, but she simply would not allow Kyle to be turned into one of those street fighters who turned up on the nightly news, either as killer or victim.

The distant sound that had been niggling at the edge of her awareness swelled to a roar, and she looked up to see a sleek jet, painted in the red-and-gray color scheme of Redstone Inc. She thought it looked like the same one that had ferried her here from California, and wondered if Tess Machado was flying it. She had liked the charming woman with dark, pixie-cut hair and the lovely smile. It had been an experience unlike any she'd ever had; the novelty of leaving when it was convenient for her, of knowing the plane would wait if she was late, and sheer amazement at the amenities. And Tess had told her Josh—anyone who'd worked for Redstone more than a year seemed to call him that—hadn't gone for the extreme luxury he produced for other customers; he'd spent his money in the avionics, the instruments and in extra training for his pilots.

Even Kyle had forgotten his anger in the thrill of the ride on the powerful jet, and for the length of the ride at least, they'd been close once more as he excitedly pointed things out to her. He'd even thanked her when she'd negotiated with Tess to allow him a brief period in the cockpit. She knew he would enjoy it, and besides, it couldn't hurt for him to see the pilot was female.

As the jet headed for the landing strip, Paige glanced at her watch. The point man, it seemed, was right on time; the staff meeting was set to begin in an hour. Everything she'd ever seen connected to Redstone seemed to run like clockwork, although she was sure there had to be glitches in at least some of their huge undertakings. But that's what this guy was here for, she thought. To smooth out the bumps in these last days before the Redstone Bay Resort opened for business.

She closed her journal and stood up. The mild breeze played with the hem of her new, tropical-print dress, an indulgence she had allowed herself the day after she'd accepted the job offer that had brought her here. She rarely wore it—she had to be too careful as a redhead in a land of tropical sun—but she'd put it on today because she needed the confidence the flattering dress gave her.

And speaking of that job, she told herself, she'd better take the short time she had to go over her papers once more. She doubted the man would want to delve into her lesson plans, but it had been a few years since she'd taught, and Joshua Redstone had taken a chance on her, so she wanted to be completely prepared just in case. She was happy with how her students had adapted so far.

Except for the one student she'd known was going to be a problem from the beginning, a certain angry, recalcitrant fifteen-year-old. Kyle alone sapped at her energy, and she wasn't sure she was up to adding twenty-six other kids into the mix. But she had no choice.

After one final glance over her schedules and plans, she gathered everything up and put it into her tote bag. It would take about five minutes for her to walk to the main building from their bungalow. She'd let him pick it out from the ones available for staff, hoping it would make him less resistant to being here. It hadn't helped much—she suspected he'd picked this one because it was farthest from the schoolhouse and would be the most inconvenient for her.

But she'd taken his choice gracefully, exclaiming on the lovely view of the water and closeness to the perfect beach, as if it were the one she would have chosen herself. That her reaction only made him angrier seemed proof of her suspicions, and she knew then that when you came to paradise, you could still carry your own hell with you.

Rider studied himself in the mirror for a moment, decided his tie was even enough, and reached for his suit coat. Later he would change into more casual clothes. He'd found it helped loosen people up, that they talked more easily to a guy in jeans or khakis. Maybe he'd even pull out that Hawaiian-style shirt Josh had given him. He'd thought at the time the shirt was a joke, but then wondered if maybe it was his boss's way of telling him once more to lighten up and relax. Of course, it had been Josh who'd had him on the run for three months straight, bouncing all over the globe to keep up with various projects.

He rubbed at his eyes, knowing he'd need about ten hours' sleep to help the redness. But other than that he looked fairly presentable now that he'd had a shower and tried out the hotel barber, who had arrived a couple of days ago to set up shop and get the staff in shape. Not that Josh cared how you wore your hair, as long as it was clean and neat. Rider had seen the single photograph that had survived from the founder of Redstone's mysterious youth, and the teenager with the intense eyes and the long mane of dark hair didn't seem all that far removed from the business powerhouse Rider knew now.

He stepped outside his room just as Barry Rutherford, the cherub-faced, slightly fussy project manager, was arriving.

"I'm sorry I wasn't here to greet you, Mr. Rider. I'll show you to the dining room," he said formally, referring to the large room utilized by the staff. Redstone Bay was specifically designed not to handle conferences or large meetings, it was for people to get away and unwind.

"Just 'Rider,' please, Barry," he said. "And I probably

can find it. I think I had the plans memorized before construction even started." He gave Barry a crooked grin. "Let me try, anyway, since you're here to save me if I get lost."

Barry smiled tentatively this time when he spoke. "I really am sorry I wasn't here when you arrived."

"What fire were you putting out?" Rider asked with another grin, this time one of commiseration and understanding.

"A small one, really. Our facilities director was called home for an emergency, and I had to assign someone to handle the job."

Rider headed down the hall toward the elevator. "Will he be back in time?"

"I don't know, I'm afraid. It's something to do with the problems on Arethusa. So I'm going to work out a schedule to cover in case he's unable to return right away."

"Good," Rider said with a nod, although he was frowning inwardly. Suddenly Arethusa didn't seem quite so distant.

But the resort itself was looking good. True, there were materials scattered about and workers scurrying, but he was used to that. He'd learned long ago to look past the surface chaos and see truly how close they were to being ready. And Redstone Bay was close.

"What's hanging besides polish work?" he asked.

"Nothing, really," Barry said proudly. "All the major projects are done."

"What about off-site? The staff housing, the school?"

"The only bungalows not completed are the ones where the occupants can't make up their minds what color they want," Barry said with a chuckle. "The school was finished last month, and is already in operation."

"Any changes?"

He shook his head. "None needed. Somebody spec'ed it out perfectly."

Rider wondered if the man was trying to butter him up;

he must know Rider had been the one who had made the final changes on the plans and equipment list for the small schoolhouse.

"The man's a bit manic about education," Rider said, referring to the passion all of Josh's people knew about.

"It keeps people happy, being able to work here and keep their kids with them."

"And Redstone likes happy people," Rider intoned, quoting the mantra that they all laughed at but lived by, knowing that as far as employers went they were with one of the best. The formula Josh had stuck to for years still worked; he hired top-notch people, paid them well and let them run.

Rider found his way to the dining room as easily as he'd hoped. It was nearly full; the staff would eat at different times, so it would rarely be this packed again. Rider declined Barry's offer to introduce him to the gathered crowd, many of whom had noticed their entrance and suspended conversation.

"I don't want this to be that formal," he explained. "I'm not the boss checking up on the employees."

Barry nodded. "Here's the roster," he said, handing Rider a small sheaf of papers. "And your master card-key." Rider took the papers and slipped the key into a pocket; he knew the key, which would override any lock in the resort, was the symbol that the project manager considered all parts of the hotel ready for official inspection. It had become a tradition of sorts, and Rider knew that as long as he got that key within eight hours of his arrival, chances were things would be okay.

He stepped up to the small podium. It didn't take long for the silence to spread. When they were all watching him he said, "I'm Noah Rider, the project coordinator, and I'm here to tell you if you don't like the uniforms, it's too late."

Laughter rippled through the room, as he'd hoped it

would; they'd all had a chance to give their input and vote on what the uniforms should be.

"I haven't had much time to look around yet," he went on, "but what I can see looks good. That's not to say there aren't some problems, there always are. That's what I'm here to help with. But everything's coming together nicely, you've all obviously done your jobs well, and Redstone Bay is lucky to have you."

A burst of cheers and whistles greeted that.

"That said, anyone have any problems that need to be dealt with before opening day?"

"We need a new movie service," somebody called out. "This one just runs the same old stuff over and over."

Rider grinned. "Just so happens I brought along a really big satellite dish. Anybody know how to set one of those puppies up?"

Laughter and cheers met that as well. When no other complaints arose, he nodded in satisfaction.

On some other level of his mind, beneath the part that was handling the speaking task, he registered that there was a redhead in the back row. She snagged his attention, as any woman with hair of that particular rich, autumn-leaves shade did. Even after five years.

It wasn't that he thought about it a lot. It was not, after all, his finest hour, and he didn't like dwelling on it. In fact, in a life that held few regrets, that one woman stood as an eternal torch of reproach.

He shook off the memory and began again, scanning the room, trying to make eye contact with everyone. "I hope to meet with you all over the next ten days, and I want you to feel free to bring up anything you want. Some of the best ideas come from you, out on the front line, and that's what I'm here for."

It was a motivational statement, Rider knew, but it was also true, and Redstone believed in it. And the staff responded, nodding as they turned and glanced at each other.

There was a reason Redstone was consistently in the top ten on lists of best places to work.

"Doesn't matter if it's business or personal, I—"

Rider was only vaguely aware he'd stopped talking. Or that he was staring. A beefy, broad-shouldered man had shifted in his seat, giving Rider a full view of the woman with the coppery hair.

It can't be.

She sat there at the very back table, staring down at folders in front of her. He silently urged her to look up, to face him so he could be sure. But she didn't. Or wouldn't. And he was sure, anyway. He knew he couldn't mistake the long, thick braid of hair, the line of her cheekbones, the tilt of her nose. He knew if she looked up, her eyes would be that rich, cinnamon-brown. He knew it.

But it can't be.

He lifted the now-forgotten page of statistics and grabbed at the personnel roster Barry had given him. He scanned it quickly and let out a sigh of relief; her name wasn't there. It was a fluke, just a resemblance. He'd reacted out of guilt, that's all.

Steady again, he moved to slip the roster back beneath his page of notes. It snagged on something, and he reached to free it from the small piece of paper stapled to the back of the roster.

He glimpsed the last few words on the note before his page pulled clear. He grabbed at it, tearing it loose from the staple. And there it was, immutable and real. The news that the teacher had arrived nearly a month ago to get the island school up and running before the opening. The teacher. Paige Cooper.

He'd hoped never to see her again. He'd hungered to see her again. He'd never resolved the contradiction. And now the contradiction was sitting in front of him.

The only woman who had ever made him throw whatever decency and common sense he had out the window.

The only woman who could shame him with just a look.

The only woman who had ever made him ache for her in so many ways he couldn't even count them all.

Paige Cooper, sitting there, refusing to look at him, reminding him all the more of what he'd done the last time he'd seen her. He remembered his earlier assessment, and decided he must have really ticked off whatever god was in charge of his fate at the moment.

The ship he'd thought was going to have a smooth sailing had just encountered a reef.

Chapter 2

He had a roomful of people staring at him, and Rider couldn't for the life of him remember what he'd been going to say. He wasn't at a total loss often enough to have learned how to deal with it well, so he knew he was fumbling now. He took refuge in the numbers and details he could spout without thought and began the rundown while his mind raced.

He shouldn't have been so surprised. It was a very Joshua-like thing to do, to hire the widow of one of his people. Especially since Phil Cooper had been killed while working for Redstone. Even though the man hadn't been one of Redstone's hires originally—he'd been a vice president of a purchased company—Josh didn't make a habit of wholesale firings at new acquisitions.

I would have fired him, Rider thought, anger spiking even after all this time. But he knew his feelings were biased. The Redstone investigation into Cooper's death had been, as usual, thorough and deep. In fact, the deepest one he'd ever seen, because the plane had been brought down over Portugal by a terrorist bomb. After five years they still didn't know exactly who had done it, they'd only succeeded in narrowing down the possibilities. And discovering that Cooper had left his widow in unpleasant, if not dire, straits.

Rider knew the truth about why Phil Cooper had been on that plane. If he hadn't, he would have felt only a vague sorrow at the death of a man he'd hardly known. And only a pity-tinged sympathy for his wife.

But instead...

With an effort he shoved his thoughts aside. He finished acknowledging the impressive list of things accomplished since construction had started. And finally remembered where he'd been before he'd gotten derailed.

"As I was saying before jet lag caught up with me," he joked, "whatever you have to say, I'm here to listen. Those of you who have worked for Redstone, you know I mean it. Those of you who are just starting out, welcome."

He started to move away from the podium, then turned back. "Oh, did I mention the party? We'll be having it two days before the opening." He managed a grin. "Two days, because we expect you to enjoy it so much it'll take that long to clean up for the opening."

A rather raucous round of applause greeted that statement, loudest from those who had worked at a Redstone resort before and knew that they definitely knew how to throw a party.

Rider waved in recognition of the good cheer and left the small lectern. The moment his mind was freed from the task of conducting the meeting, it leaped back to the subject he'd tried to suppress.

Paige Cooper. Here. Unavoidably here.

He let out a compressed breath. He'd long ago given up trying to convince himself that what he'd felt five years before was just sympathy. He'd felt a lot more than that. And what he'd felt had led him to actions so uncharacteristic that he'd shocked himself. He still couldn't quite believe it.

And if his reaction just now was any indication, those feelings had only been in hibernation.

His smooth-sailing ship, he thought grimly, had just run aground.

I should have known, Paige moaned inwardly. How could it not have even occurred to me that it would be him?

She barely managed to gather up her papers, and nearly dropped the tote bag in her haste. She dodged out of the dining room and headed for the outer door at the fastest pace she could manage without running and drawing attention. Once outside she slowed, pressing her fingers to her face, wishing for an icy-cold breeze. Her fingers were cooler than her overheated cheeks, but not cool enough. Ice, she thought. Ice would be good.

"You idiot," she muttered to herself. "You're such a fool."

She knew, had known even back then, that Noah Rider was one of Redstone's premiere point men. That he ran all over the world, setting up new operations, finalizing things. So why on earth hadn't she realized there was a good chance the exec sent to oversee the final stages of Redstone Bay would be him? True, she'd been busy, her classes had started barely a week after she'd arrived so the kids would be in the routine by the time the resort opened, so there had been little chance for her to hear his name mentioned, but still—

"Paige? You all right?" Miranda Mayfield, head of technical services and mother of two of her students, put a hand on her shoulder.

"Fine. Thank you." She sounded completely unconvincing, even to herself. Miranda looked doubtful, and Paige tried to pull herself together. "It must have been the crowd," she said. "I've gotten used to the quiet here."

Miranda smiled. "It is that, isn't it? Almost makes up for those rascals you're trying to teach."

Paige managed a smile. "They're good kids." Except for mine, at the moment, she amended silently.

"They like you. And you're giving attention to all of them, despite the difference in ages. All the parents are pleased. We know that can't be easy to accomplish."

"Thank you," Paige said again, meaning it this time. It was sweet of Miranda to tell her that.

When the woman had gone, Paige took in a deep breath of the balmy air. She was steadier now. Steady enough to marvel at how shaken she had felt just moments ago.

But perhaps it wasn't so surprising. Not when she'd just been faced with the man who'd inspired her to the most impulsive thing she'd ever done in her generally traditional life. Her husband's body not even brought home yet, and she'd shared a passionate embrace with a man she barely knew. An embrace that could easily have led to more, had the arrival of her son not interrupted them. Her recollection of that time wasn't clear, was mercifully lost in a sort of fog, but that one vivid, shocking memory was forever seared into her mind.

She had been able, since then, to rationalize her actions. Given the circumstances—all of them—she obviously hadn't been herself. But there was no analyzing away her reaction to the man. What she'd done, practically throwing herself at him, might have arisen out of her emotional state, but her response to him, to his mouth, to his hands on her, had been purely physical and unlike anything she'd ever known before or since.

And if she'd succeeded over the past five years in pushing him out of her mind, it had been made clear to her just now that her body remembered him perfectly. So perfectly it had nearly forgotten how to breathe when he'd walked into the room.

It made no sense. She knew who he was, what he was,

that he was a globe-trotter of epic proportion. That alone should be enough to send her scurrying; she'd been down that road once and still carried the scars. But instead she had been drawn, aware not only of the piercing blue of his eyes and the male strength of his jaw but the empathy she'd seen in his eyes and the gentle touch of hands that somehow seemed to ease the pain.

And if the jump of her heart just now and the pounding that had followed when she had realized it really was him were any indication, she was still drawn. Powerfully. Painfully.

Foolishly. That above all. Noah Rider was many things, including good-looking, smart, trusted by the shrewd and brilliant Joshua Redstone, and a high-powered executive, just as her late husband had been. What he was not was a man for a woman like her. Or perhaps any woman. She'd heard his work came first, last and in between.

She heard the door open behind her again and wished she'd gone before the motherly Miranda had come back to check on her again. With a "Really, I'm fine" on her lips she began to turn. But she froze; the footsteps she heard did not belong to the petite, usually high-heeled Miranda. They were heavier, more solid. Male. Yes, definitely male.

She should truly have run when she'd had the chance.

The footsteps came to a halt behind her. Every muscle in her body seemed to tighten as she waited, holding her breath. It could be anyone, but she knew as clearly as if she'd turned to look who it was.

The silence spun out for a long, aching moment.

"Paige?"

She let out the breath she'd been holding, in a long, inaudible sigh. It took every bit of nerve she had to do it, but she turned to face him.

"Hello, Noah," she said, softer than she would have liked, but more evenly than she'd expected. And then regretted it, when a faint flicker in those eyes reminded her he was usually referred to as Rider by everyone else.

For a long moment he just stood there, staring at her. He was as big as she remembered, at least six feet, a good eight inches taller than she. His hair was just as dark, and he wore the same kind of conservative gray suit—although because of the tropical locale, lighter weight this time—he had worn the last time she'd seen him.

And he still looked so incredibly strong. She had almost convinced herself that she'd only thought he was because she herself had been feeling so wobbly and weak at the time. But now she knew better.

"I didn't know you would be here," he said abruptly, the words coming out in a rush.

She took another quick, steadying breath to be sure her voice would come out normally.

"And I didn't know the project coordinator would be you. Although I suppose I should have," she added honestly.

Only after she'd spoken did the implication of his first words sink in. *I didn't know you would be here.* Meaning what? That if he had, he wouldn't have come? Would have made them send someone else? Had she embarrassed him that much, made him feel so awkward he would actually let it get in the way of his work? The thought made her so hideously self-conscious that she scrambled to fill the silence.

"I wanted to tell you—the project coordinator, I mean, that the school is really wonderful. You did an excellent job planning the modernization."

He blinked once, his brows furrowed slightly, then he seemed to relax. So he *had* felt awkward, she thought. No doubt he was glad she'd brought up something so...safe.

"Keeping your family with you is one of the perks of working for Redstone."

"So I've been told," she said. Phil had never wanted to avail himself of that option.

But she also knew from the staff—whenever they weren't talking about the problems brewing in nearby Arethusa—that the staff housing and the school were directly overseen by the coordinator. "But I know the coordinator made several changes and additions to the school plans, and they've worked out very well for the children."

His mouth quirked at one corner. "I figured the indoor plumbing would be a hit."

Paige blushed, wondering if he was inwardly laughing at her. Perhaps he always had been. Poor, new widow, throwing herself at the first man who tried to comfort her. Maybe that's all she was to him, a slightly embarrassing, mostly pitiful memory. She couldn't blame him for that. It's how she thought of herself back then, too. But she was stronger now. Much stronger. He'd no longer find much trace of the wobbly, uncertain woman she'd been in those days after Phil's death.

"I had more in mind the computer center," she said, making her voice match her more determined thoughts. "The kids are already using it, even ones who've never seen a computer before."

One dark brow lowered, as if at the new intonation in her words. "I'm glad to hear that. There was some…discussion over the extra construction it took for the wiring."

She read between the lines and said, "Thank you for fighting for it, then."

He shrugged. "Wasn't much of a fight. They knew if it got all the way to Josh, he'd approve it." His forehead creased. "Is your son with you?"

"Yes and no," Paige said wryly, then regretted the words. Her problems with Kyle weren't something she wanted to discuss, least of all with this man.

"Does that mean he's here physically but not mentally?"

"Exactly," she said, surprised he'd gotten her meaning so quickly. "He's not happy with me for making him leave L.A."

Rider scanned the lovely vista before them, inviting pathways through gently waving palm trees, stretching down to a pristine white beach.

"One man's paradise is another man's hell," he said softly.

He'd surprised her again. "And L.A. was this mother's hell," she said, her voice rather sharp. "Kyle was headed for serious trouble, and I was not going to let it happen."

His gaze snapped back to her. "He never came around? After he found out...?"

He paused, clearly uncomfortable. She'd been so focused on the stupid things she'd done, she'd forgotten Rider had met Kyle, however briefly, in the days he'd been with her after the crash. And that his concern had stretched to both of them. Perhaps if she'd been more aware of that, she would have seen that he'd merely been being kind, not sending an invitation to the widow.

And suddenly she knew she couldn't go on like this. If she were to get through the time he would be here, she couldn't handle the strain of either trying to dodge him or feeling this horrible knot in her stomach every time she saw him. Not on top of dealing with Kyle and keeping up with her students.

She bit her lip, not knowing how to say it, then finally just blurted it out. "Could we talk?"

His brows furrowed for a split second, in what she thought was a flinch. "Is that talk with a capital *T*?"

The woman she'd once been might have given up. Might have ignored the elephant in the kitchen, hoping it would magically vanish, as she had done with too much else. The woman she was trying to be would not.

"Let's just say—" she looked around at the people who

had exited the meeting and were now milling about, some glancing their way "—that I don't want to do it here."

"Paige, is this necessary?"

She hadn't really considered that this might be as distasteful to him as to her. He'd probably managed to forget all about that night, until he'd walked into that meeting and seen her, the painful reminder.

It would be better for both of them, she thought. She was sure of that. "It's necessary for me," she insisted.

He let out an audible breath. "All right. I've got meetings the rest of the day. What about dinner?"

She frowned; that sounded too much like a social occasion, and while this wasn't really business—except the unfinished, personal kind—she didn't feel comfortable with the implications of a formal dinner engagement.

"I'm sorry," he said stiffly when she didn't answer. "I should have realized you wouldn't want to do that. Later this evening then?"

"Fine," she said, wondering why he suddenly sounded so odd.

He appeared to be thinking for a moment. "The overlook?"

The deck built out over the steepest slope down to the beach would most likely be private enough. And convenient, she thought sourly, if she decided to jump off.

"Fine," she repeated. "You just got here, do you know where it is?"

"Theoretically, from the plans. I need to check it out in person, anyway."

He sounded more natural now, but still stiffer than before. Dreading this, she assumed. "It won't take long," she assured him. "Eight?"

"Fine." He echoed her acceptance.

"All right." She became suddenly aware that several of the people from the meeting were still lingering, and she realized they must be waiting for him. "I'd better go. People are waiting to speak to you, I think."

"Seems to be my lot in life today," he muttered.

She winced inwardly, but said nothing as she turned and hurried back toward her bungalow. After tonight it would truly be over. She would deliver her long-overdue apology, he would hopefully accept it when he understood she was as embarrassed as he, and they could both put that night behind them.

"I'm going with you."

"No," Paige said firmly. "You're not."

Kyle eyed her stubbornly from beneath the old, dirty baseball cap he still insisted on wearing backward despite the brilliant flood of sunlight here. The two earrings that pierced his left earlobe glinted, one gold, one silver and black. The second was a rather grim representation of a skull she hated but hadn't made an issue of, for fear it would make him determined to keep wearing it whether he really wanted to or not.

"Why not?"

"To start with, you weren't asked. Mr. Rider and I have things to talk about."

"You're going to talk about Dad, aren't you? So I want to go. He knew him. I want to ask him some things."

"We have school business to talk about." That much was true; she did want to give him at least a brief report on the school and the students' progress. "Besides, he didn't know your father well at all."

"How do you know?"

"Because he said so. Mr. Rider only met him briefly a couple of times."

"Then why did they send him, after he died?"

She'd wondered that on more than one occasion herself. Wondered what would have happened—or not happened—if they'd sent someone else.

"I don't know. Perhaps I'll ask him."

She gathered up the lightweight blue shawl to toss over her shoulders; the breeze had been picking up at night lately, and while it was hardly cold, it could be cool on bare arms. At the door she paused and looked back at her son.

"Don't forget you've got that history assignment, and the next chapter of *Beowulf* to read."

She thought he swore under his breath, but wasn't sure enough to call him on it. "Bad enough to have to go to school, but living with the teacher sucks."

"You've been living with a teacher all your life," she pointed out.

"Yeah, but you weren't *my* teacher."

She gave him a long, steady look. "I tried to be," she said. "About the things that really count, at least."

He turned and walked away, into his bedroom, without a word. He'd taken to doing that recently, walking away from any discussion he didn't want to have. She was going to have to call him on that soon, convince him that running away from the unpleasant didn't work. She was certainly living proof of that.

As she walked toward the lookout, she rehearsed in her mind yet again what she would say. There was no easy way to apologize for having so embarrassed them both, and having thought about how she would do it countless times hadn't helped.

How did you apologize for something like that? The man had been there as a representative of her husband's company, he'd been doing his job, nothing more. They'd been kind enough to send him to see if she was all right or needed anything they could provide. Her emotional state had been so very tangled and fragile, and she had clung to him. And he had let her, comforting her, giving her his strong arm to lean on and broad shoulder to cry on. He'd helped her through the ugly process, even made the arrangements to have Phil's remains shipped home on one of Redstone's own planes.

For nearly two weeks he'd been there to help. And then, one night after a nasty emotional outburst from the grieving Kyle, a night when she'd felt more alone than she ever had before, she'd leaned on his strength once more. He'd held her, soothed her…but when she'd looked up into his eyes she'd thought she'd seen something more, something warm and hungry.

She'd responded to that look, imagined or not, with a speed and urgency that had astounded her even as it was happening. The next thing she knew she was kissing him. Hotly, deeply, in a way that made her blush at the memory even now, five years later. And the fact that he kissed her back, the fact that after a few moments his strong hands had begun to caress her, to rouse in her startling sensations that made her shiver, didn't ameliorate her own responsibility for what had happened.

And what might have happened, had Kyle not just then slammed back into the house, fortunately through the kitchen door, giving them time to recover before he walked in on them. If she thought he was angry with her now, she could only imagine how he might have felt had he seen his mother kissing another man before his father's body was even home, let alone buried.

Of course, Kyle didn't know what she knew. At least she'd managed to keep that from him. It hadn't been an easy choice, but it was the only one she could make. Her son had already been in agony. She couldn't risk any further damage.

Rider was there, waiting for her. She stopped a distance away, looking at him silhouetted against the fading light. He was leaning forward, hands braced on the railing, staring out at the sea. The light breeze caught his shirt and swirled it. He'd changed into casual clothes, she saw. Khaki pants, it looked like, and a Hawaiian-style shirt in muted colors. Navy-blue and tan, the same shade as the khakis, she thought. And realized with a little jolt she'd never seen him, this man who had taken up permanent residence in her memory, in anything other than a suit. Until now.

He seemed to sense her presence and turned. She started up the last few steps and walked out onto the deck. Just say it and get it over with, she told herself. Just apologize. Just do it.

Instead, when she reached him she found herself asking inanely, "So, does it meet your standards?"

There was a second before he answered, and she wondered if she'd startled him, if he'd been expecting her to plunge right into the emotional depths. Since that had been her plan, she couldn't blame him; it wasn't his fault that she'd chickened out at the last second.

"It's solid. Well built, good materials."

She couldn't help the half laugh that escaped her. "Most people would be raving about the view."

He shrugged. "It takes advantage of it."

She sighed. "I suppose when you've seen views all over the world, it takes more to impress you."

He gave her a puzzled look. "You must have seen a place or two."

"Nope. Never been out of California, until now."

His puzzlement shifted to a frown. "But your husband traveled extensively."

"Yes. Alone." Maybe, she added bitterly to herself.

"You never went with him?"

"No. With Kyle so young, I preferred it that way." Not that he would have wanted me along, anyway.

"And now you've traveled halfway around the world."

"I had no choice."

He looked at her for a long, silent moment. "So you gave up your life to move your son. That's quite a sacrifice."

Her eyes widened. "Not many would see coming here as a sacrifice."

"Sacrifice is in the reasons not the setting," he said.

She considered what he said. "That's rather profound."

He only shrugged. For a moment the only sound was the rustle of the palm fronds and the more distant sound of the surf from below. It was time, she told herself. Time to get it done. She opened her mouth to speak, to at last say she was sorry.

"Okay, let's get it over with," he said, before she'd gotten a word out. "I'm sorry. It should never have happened."

She gaped at him as he spoke the words she'd opened her own mouth to say.

"What?" she finally managed.

"I'm apologizing, all right?" He nearly snapped it out. "It's been eating at me for five years, so I'm apologizing. I took advantage. I'm a jerk and a slime and an idiot, and all the rotten things you've probably been calling me all this time."

She stared at him. "That," she barely managed to squeak out, "is what I've been calling *myself* for the past five years."

Chapter 3

Paige felt utterly bewildered. But there could be no doubt—he'd said it so adamantly. The man she'd wanted to apologize to for so long was instead apologizing to her.

She heard an odd little chiming sound.

"Damn," he muttered under his breath. "Excuse me," he said to her; she wasn't sure if it was for the curse or the interruption. He reached into a shirt pocket that had looked empty and pulled out the smallest cell phone she'd ever seen. He pushed a button and said sharply, "Rider."

He listened for a moment, his mouth tightening. Finally he advised the caller he would be down in a few minutes, and disconnected. He slipped the tiny phone back into the upper pocket.

"Bad news?" she asked.

"Minor problem. I'll deal with it after…we're finished here."

That brought her back sharply to the realization that had so startled her. "Noah, I can't believe you're apologizing to me after what I did! I'm the one who jumped all over you, when all you were trying to do was be helpful.''

"Helpful?" Both dark brows shot up. "Is that what you thought?"

"I know you were just trying to comfort me, and then I—"

"I knew you were vulnerable, I knew you were confused, and I let it happen, anyway." He grimaced but went on flatly. "It was my fault. I was supposed to take care of you, not..." His voice trailed off as he shook his head in obvious disgust.

"But I started it," she protested.

"You weren't thinking straight. Under the circumstances you can hardly be blamed."

"But you can?" she asked, steadier now.

"I hadn't just been through an emotional meat grinder. Yes, I can be blamed all right."

Paige felt as if her world had tilted slightly on its axis. She'd worked up to this, had planned it for the day she might see him again, had even considered making it happen, even if she had to call Redstone and make an appointment. Only to find now that he had felt the same way. And suddenly she realized the reason he'd looked so odd when he'd suggested dinner and she'd reacted negatively—when he'd said he should have known she wouldn't want to do that, he'd been thinking she wouldn't want to have dinner with a man who had, in his view, treated her so badly.

If you only knew, she thought. On her scale of being treated badly, that kiss didn't even make the top million.

"You're right about one thing, though," he said after a moment. "This should have been done long ago. I owed you that much."

"I owed you a lot more. I don't think I'd have gotten through that time if you hadn't been there."

His mouth twisted. "Nice to know I didn't completely fall down on the job."

That reminded her. "Tell me something, will you? Why did they send you back then? Why not somebody from, I don't know, personnel, maybe?"

He shrugged. "I'd just been in Portugal a few weeks before. I knew some people, people I could call if there were any problems with...arrangements. But there weren't, really. They were as horrified as the rest of the world, more so since the plane had gone down in their country. They went out of their way to help."

As simple as that. As simply as that a practical choice was made, and her life was changed forever.

Paige drew in a deep breath of the night air, savored the scent of the night-blooming flowers that had been carefully planted around the grounds. Some sweet, some spicy, it was the kind of perfume that would never be matched by the hand of man in a laboratory.

Somehow the knowledge that he had felt nearly as bad as she enabled her to finish what she'd come here to do.

"If we're going to work together while you're here, we have to put this behind us," she began. "We can't both go on feeling guilty about it."

"Wanna bet?"

The words were negative, but his tone was much lighter, and Paige nearly smiled. "Can we forget about it and go on?"

"Forget that I took advantage of you?"

"You didn't, but I'll allow you that if you accept I was the initiator and a willing participant."

He closed his eyes, as if her words had caused him pain. After a moment he opened them again. "I suppose it's going to be impossible to do what we have to do here if we can't get past it."

"It will be for me," she admitted.

"So we both made mistakes, now we go on?"

"Right."

He turned to look back out over the calm, warm sea. She heard him take a couple of deep breaths.

"All right. We start over," he said finally.

"Hello, Noah Rider. I'm Paige Cooper," she answered.

He turned back to her then. An odd expression was on his face, and an odder half smile curved his mouth. That mouth she'd spent five years trying to forget.

"Hello, Paige Cooper," he said. "Nice to meet you."

Rider walked down the long hallway to the administrative offices of the hotel. He'd kept Barry waiting longer than he'd wanted to, but he'd had to finish with Paige.

Finish with Paige.

That was something he'd been hoping for for five years now. To conclude what had felt like unfinished business. Or at the least, unatoned-for business. So why didn't he feel relieved, now that the air had been cleared, apologies—however unexpected hers had been—made, and an agreement reached that they would forget and move on?

Forget. Right. Not likely. He had thought it would be over now. That after he'd apologized to her, she would have forgiven him, and they could have gone on, comfortable in the knowledge that they would rarely, if ever, see each other again once he left here. It should have been easy.

But it wasn't. Not a damned thing had changed. Except now she was right here, within reach.

So now what? He was supposed to just smile and walk around cheerfully as if it had never happened? Pretend he'd never met her before this day, that she hadn't been a warm, taunting image in the back of his mind since even before the night he'd made himself walk away from her?

His cell phone rang again.

"Rider."

"Sir?" The voice was tentative. "This is Miranda Mayfield, in tech services? I know it's after hours, but you did say to let you know when the test data on the standby generators was finished.''

''Relax, Miranda. There's no such thing as after hours for me while I'm here. Drop it off in my temporary office, will you? Then go home.''

''Thanks, Mr. Rider.''

He slipped the phone back in his pocket just as he reached Barry Rutherford's office. The door was open, and the man was still at his desk. Out of courtesy Rider tapped on the doorjamb rather than just striding in. He might outrank the man in the general scheme of things, but Redstone Bay was Rutherford's bailiwick, and would be long after Rider was gone.

''So what's that bad news?''

''I just hung up with Bohio's family,'' Barry said. ''What I'd feared is true. He's not coming back.''

''Because?''

''Sadly, that emergency he left for was the death of his brother.''

Rider frowned. ''Did you tell him we'd hold the job for him, as long as he needed?''

''I'm afraid I wasn't able to speak to him directly. He's no longer there.''

Rider studied the older man's face for a moment. ''Do I need to sit down for this?''

''As you wish. It's not pretty, but not unusual of late. Bohio's brother was in the army. He was killed in a skirmish with the rebel forces on Arethusa. Bohio has decided he must help the army hunt down those responsible.''

Rider's mouth twisted. In all his travels he'd more than once been close to a restless part of the world. He hadn't liked it then and he didn't now. He dealt with it when he had to, but that didn't mean he enjoyed it.

''And he's already gone?'' he asked.

Barry nodded.

So, no chance to try to talk him out of it. Not that he

could have, but it would have been nice to try. But he could understand—intellectually, anyway, because he'd never had to face such a decision himself—that Bohio had felt he had to do this.

"See if the family needs anything," he told Barry.

"I will. As for his job, we'll need somebody fairly soon to replace him."

Rider gave the man a wry smile. "You're a master of understatement, Barry. I'm sure Redstone has someone they could send out temporarily. But first, are there any possibilities already here?"

Barry frowned. "You mean, someone who could take over? No one with his training and credentials."

"What about any bright lights? Somebody who's shown some knowledge or initiative?"

Barry thought for a moment. He opened his mouth as if to speak, then shut it again.

"What?" Rider asked.

The man shook his head. "No, he's too young."

"Who?"

"Elan Kiskeya. A local. He's been helping Bohio, so he knows the systems, and he's got a knack for mechanical things, but…"

"Does he have the drive?"

"He's always asking for more to do, but he's only twenty-four."

"I was twenty-six when Josh Redstone gave me a shot at your position on the San Juan Islands project," Rider said. "I'd never done anything that big before. I worked harder than I ever had in my life, to prove I could do it."

It had also been nerve-racking as hell, San Juan being Redstone's first resort venture. But now it was a cornerstone of the resort end of the business, and Rider knew it was why he was where he was today.

"He would have to learn a great deal very quickly," Barry warned.

"Is there a good staff in place? I haven't gotten to that part of the report yet."

Barry nodded. "Very good. Bohio picked good people. Including Kiskeya. Do you wish to talk to him?"

"Let's bring him in tomorrow so we can discuss it. But it's going to affect you the most, since you may have to help him along, so the final decision is yours. If you don't think he can cut it, we'll send for help."

Barry looked a bit relieved. "All right."

Rider smiled. "Steamrollering people from the top isn't the Redstone style."

The man chuckled. "Did I look that worried?"

"Just a little."

"I'll have Kiskeya come in first thing in the morning, if that works for you?"

"Sooner the better. He's going to need all the time he can get. And let's hope we don't lose anybody else."

On his way back to the small suite set aside for visiting Redstone personnel, Rider's thoughts played back those moments in the dining room meeting when he'd seen Paige, doubted his own eyes, then seen her name undeniably written before him. But it still hadn't quite sunk in until he'd caught up with her outside. But there, with her hair a fiery beacon in the setting tropical sun, he was sure. She looked just as he remembered so vividly. She'd been standing with her arms drawn in tightly, as if she'd been as shaken as he by the unexpected encounter. And when she'd begun to chatter about the improvements to the schoolhouse, as if desperate for any diversion, he'd been sure of it. She was as rattled as he was.

He should be fine now, he argued to himself as he closed the suite door behind him. They'd talked it out, it was over, time to move on. He still felt utterly responsible for what had happened that night—he supposed there were worse things than kissing and pawing a distraught widow, though it was surely one of the worst things he'd ever done—but was at least relieved to know that she didn't hate him or blame him.

He pulled off his shirt and tossed it over the back of a chair. He should be exhausted; his day had become a marathon. But instead he felt strangely wired. He kicked off his shoes, then looked at the stocked minibar consideringly. He was more inclined to put on his running shoes and go out for a late-night jog. But he decided against it; his memory for plans and layouts was good, and there was nearly a full moon, but he'd only physically been here once before, and inadvertently running off a cliff wasn't his idea of a good way to end a day that had already been trying enough.

He resorted to pouring a small amount of Amaretto into a glass, then wandered out onto the lanai. From here he could just see the overlook, where he and Paige had stood. He sat down on the edge of one of the chaises, then gave in to the lure, swung his legs up and leaned back. He had a lot to do in the next few days, but for now, just for now...

He woke up in the same place the next morning feeling more rested than he had in days. He wondered if it was the balmy outdoor air, the Amaretto or the simple fact that a large load had been removed from his conscience.

This island, Paige thought as she walked along the immaculate beach, watching the lap of tiny waves on the sand and the break of larger swells far beyond on the reef, had never seemed so small before. You'd think in nearly a thousand acres—and when you spent half your day in a single room with twenty-six kids—you wouldn't run into one person quite so often. But she seemed to have run into Noah Rider quite a bit in the past two days. True, it was a weekend, and once she'd graded some essays and corrected some math papers she'd had the rest of Saturday and now all of Sunday free to wander, but she'd never seen any one person as often and in as many places as she'd seen him.

So maybe it was just that he was everywhere. Anywhere there was a problem he showed up. And from what she'd heard from other staff, he managed it without stepping on any toes or coming off as the big cheese so many had expected.

Paige wasn't surprised at that. Not after the gentle, kind way he'd dealt with her in her time of need. Tact was something he clearly had in abundance. She supposed it was a requirement to reach the level he had.

And she had to admit that the times she had seen him hadn't been difficult, if you didn't count her own silly anticipation anxiety. He was acting just as she would have wished, treating her just like everyone else.

And if she didn't completely like that, it was her problem. She could not—*would* not—make it his, too.

She glimpsed some activity down the beach, a gathering of people and a small boat in the water. She headed that way, curious. She knew at this late date, so close to the scheduled opening, there was no such thing as a weekend off, so whatever it was had to be related to the resort. She was still about fifty feet away when she heard the sound of a motor, and the people gathered began to back away from the boat. She saw a flash of bright colors, red, blue and yellow, and it was a moment before she realized what it was.

And then it became obvious as the colors billowed up into an arc of fabric that then soared into the air. Parasailing, she thought, and in that instant the passenger, attached by lines that seemed too insubstantial to her unpracticed eye, soared upward.

It was Noah.

She stared, certain she must have seen wrong, but she knew deep down she hadn't. She couldn't mistake his size, his solid build, and the economy of movement that had been one of the first things she'd ever noticed about him.

But why on earth? Surely this wasn't required of him.

Did he really carry his oversight so far as to risk his neck trying out the recreational offerings? He had to be hundreds of feet up by now.

Although she had to admit, as she came up to the group of spectators, it did look exciting. Very. It looked, in fact, awfully close to flying, and she wondered if it felt like that, too.

She noticed Miranda among the watchers, and the woman smiled and walked over to her.

"My boy can't wait to try that."

Paige grimaced. "I'm sure Kyle will want to do it, too. In fact, I'm surprised he's not here."

"I saw him earlier, talking to Lani over by the pool."

Paige smiled. "Well, that should keep him happy for a while."

She knew Kyle was taken with the exotically lovely island girl whose family had lived here for generations. Her mother had died at Lani DeSouza's birth, but her father had been there for her all her life, and Paige knew the girl loved him dearly. That father had also been the local population's representative at the time Redstone had bought the island a decade ago. He had been a persuasive voice then, and, she'd heard, a shrewd bargainer. And a wise one. The people all agreed, because so far Joshua Redstone had kept every promise he'd made, including a school that would accept every child on the island.

And Lani was as clever as her father. She was a pleasure to have in class, absorbing every bit of knowledge Paige provided her with an eagerness that made Paige regret the years she'd been away from teaching, although she knew students like Lani were rare. She was secretly delighted that Kyle was interested in the bright, sweet-natured girl. Of course he was far too young to be serious, but Lani couldn't help but be a good influence on him. She hoped he would follow the girl's lead; Lani could hardly wait until this summer, when she hoped to work as one of the many personal assistants, or PAs that Redstone hired to help all their guests with any and everything, from scuba diving the reef to nature hikes to finding a book in the small but well-stocked library.

"Now there's a man," Miranda said as the boat maneuvered to bring its airborne passenger back to the beach, "to keep a woman happy."

Paige nearly blushed, then silently called herself an idiot—from now on he worked for the same company she did, that's all, she told herself.

"Mr. Rider?" she asked, trying for an innocent tone.

"I sure didn't mean ol' Rudy," Miranda said with a grin, nodding toward the round, bald, very tanned head of the executive chef.

Paige giggled in spite of herself. "I don't know. He's kind of cute, in a grandfatherly sort of way."

"Well, he does make a mean fricassee, I'll give him that," Miranda said.

Paige knew Rudy Aubert had been at a large five-star hotel for years, but had jumped at the chance to oversee this smaller but no less exclusive operation. And, judging by his tan, he was soaking up island life in a big hurry.

Unlike herself, she thought, always checking that she wasn't inadvertently exposing unscreened skin to the sun that was so deadly for her fair complexion. On this lovely day she wore leggings and a long-sleeved, gauzy blouse. Even then she'd had to put sunscreen on, knowing she could burn through the fabric if she spent too much time— for her that meant anything over half an hour—out in the sun.

"So, how long have you known him?"

Paige blinked. "Mr. Rider?" Miranda gave her a look that reminded her of the way she sometimes looked at Kyle when he didn't—or refused to—see the obvious.

"Oh." She glanced over to where Rider was now safely ashore and getting out of the harness. He was grinning widely and then he laughed, clearly exhilarated. She turned back to Miranda and said carefully, "What makes you think I've ever met him before he got here?"

The look was even worse this time. "Oh, maybe because he about swallowed his tie when he spotted you in the staff meeting. And you couldn't wait to get out of there."

She considered lying, but it seemed pointless, and she didn't want to lie to this woman who was becoming a friend. There had been more than enough lies in her life.

"I knew him from...a bad time in my life. Redstone sent him to help when my husband was killed."

Instantly contrite, Miranda put her hand on Paige's arm. "Oh, honey, I'm sorry. I didn't mean to pry."

"It's all right. It was a long time ago. And it was only that I didn't expect to ever see him again. I was...startled, that's all."

Miranda patted her arm comfortingly. "Still, I'm sorry. But, my, he'd be enough to wake up any breathing woman. So tell me, why does he only go by Rider?"

"I don't know. Maybe he just doesn't like Noah."

She liked the name, and that's how she thought of him, but now she wondered why she persisted, when he'd asked everyone else to call him Rider. Maybe because he hadn't asked *her* to call him that. And her mind skittered away from figuring out the motivation behind that particular choice.

As if satisfied that Paige wasn't really a source of details on the man in question, Miranda gave up on the subject. They chatted for a couple of minutes about how her two children were doing in class, and then the woman excused herself to go find said kids and stop them from whatever trouble she knew they were up to.

Paige watched her go, feeling oddly wistful. Once she'd said similar things, said them in that same light teasing tone, knowing it was just that, teasing, and that there was little chance her sweet boy would really be in any kind of trouble.

Now there was every chance, every day, and what she'd thought would help—extricating him from the environment that had had him skating on the edge of real problems— only seemed to have made it worse. He was angrier than ever, and it showed no signs of abating. Most days she could barely get a civil word out of him.

"Paige?"

Her breath caught at the unexpected sound of his voice so close behind her. She took a half second to steady herself before she turned around. He was wearing jeans and a blue T-shirt with the Redstone logo, and she was startled at how the casual clothes suited him even better than the executive look. He looked windblown and exhilarated, his blue eyes brighter than ever.

"Have fun?" she asked.

He grinned. "It was great. Want to try?"

She glanced toward the water again, saw that somebody else was taking a turn now. The urge was there, but so was a little tingle of fear. She looked back at Rider. "I don't know," she began.

"I saw you watching. You looked like you were wondering how it felt."

"You saw me from up there?" she said, not quite believing him.

He reached out, touched her hair with his fingertips. "You stand out."

In an instant the air between them seemed charged. She held her breath, afraid to move. He drew his hand back, looking at it in surprise, as if he hadn't even realized what he was doing. He curled his fingers to his palm, and shoved on the sunglasses he'd been holding in his other hand.

"Come on," he said. "Catch a ride before they wrap it up for the day."

She looked at the current flyer, who suddenly looked

much higher than before. She wanted to try it, but a bit of shiver down her spine stopped her from immediately jumping at the chance. "I'm not sure," she said.

"You'll love it. I promise."

"And if I don't?"

"Dinner. On me. Rudy has a new dish he wants to add to the menu."

Dinner again, she thought. As neatly as that he'd put her in a corner. If she said no, he'd think she hadn't forgiven him, that she wasn't sticking to their agreement to put it behind them. And if she said yes...

If she said yes, she could end up marooned at a table with him, truly testing the strength of her resolve to not think about what had happened between them anymore.

So, you'd better love this little adventure then, she thought. "All right," she said.

As she walked beside him down the beach, Paige had the strange but persistent feeling she'd done more than just say yes to a physical flight of fancy.

Chapter 4

Noah didn't help as the operator got her into the harness, and Paige wondered if he was avoiding touching her again. He seemed to have gotten over his tense reaction. He was cheerfully encouraging her, treating her like anyone else here.

"Tomorrow we'll hook up the tandem rig," the man was telling Noah.

"Fine," Noah said, "but right now you've got one of our most valued people."

The man took the hint and concentrated on her rigging.

"Pay attention here now," Noah said with mock sternness as the man began to give her safety instructions. "I doubt very much that doing a nosedive, or drowning because you can't get out from under yards of wet fabric is in your plans for the day."

She wrinkled her nose at him. "Charming. Are you trying to make sure I don't enjoy this?"

He grinned. "Don't put it past me. Maybe I really want

that dinner. In fact, if I'm right and you do love it, you can buy. Employees' rate, of course.''

''Gee, thanks.''

And then it was time. The man signaled the driver of the boat, and the engine changed pitch. For an instant she wanted to yell at them to stop, she'd changed her mind, but it was too late. She was committed now.

She thought it would take more time or speed, but before she even realized it, she was on her way, her feet lifting off the back of the boat. Lifting so easily it stunned her. It *was* like flying, she thought, finally remembering to breathe. Or at least close to flying. The sensation without the work. But tethered to the boat below—frighteningly far below—it was also without the control.

But the sensation was amazing, the wind of their passage whipping at her braid, the literal bird's-eye view of the resort and this side of the island. She hadn't realized the coast curved so much, she thought as she looked down through her dangling feet. She could see the variations in color in the water from here, how it changed from green to aqua to deeper blue in undulating lines. And Redstone Bay Resort itself, looking as if it had always been here, subtle, blending with the landscape.

By the change in her view she realized the boat was heading back toward the beach. She could see the group of people, all staring up at her. She thought of what Noah had said, that he'd seen her from up here, and began to look for him.

It took her only a moment. Even though he wasn't the only one in a Redstone T-shirt, he stood out to her immediately. Something about the way he held himself, or the way he was watching her so intently and not chatting with those around him. Rather inanely she thought of waving, then realized she wasn't about to let go of her grip on the lines.

Even from up here, she realized rather glumly, he fascinated her. Phil had been a high-powered businessman, but for a much smaller company. In essence Noah held a much higher position, and yet he was so much more at ease with it and with himself. He didn't seem driven, just good. Nor was he arrogant, as Phil had been with people under him. Noah treated them with respect, making it clear their contributions were valued.

And for a few days, during a ghastly time of her life, he'd made her feel valued. He'd made her feel as if she were someone who deserved to be taken care of, as if there were truly people who cared about her and wanted to help her get through this. He'd been there for Redstone, but he'd made it personal, believable.

Her mind wanted to swerve down that old track, drag up again the memory of how she'd repaid him for that, but she quashed it. She felt too wonderful to tread that old road again. They'd made a pact, and she'd keep her word. Maybe she would even pay off on that bet.

This was wonderful, she thought. Indeed exhilarating. She couldn't think of anything she'd done that was more exciting than this.

Except maybe kiss Noah Rider.

She was not having much luck keeping her promise to put that behind her, she thought wryly. But at least she could make sure he didn't know that.

She felt the change as the boat began to slow. She was sorry it was over, but that passed as she concentrated on what the man had told her about landing. As it turned out, she drifted down easily, slowly enough that she could even enjoy it. She ended up a bit off target from where they'd told her she'd land, but Noah was there, waiting. And when she hit, barely hard enough to stagger her, he was there to steady her, to keep her clear of the chaos of lines and sail.

Just as he had five years ago, he kept her balanced and safe.

She drew in a deep breath, knowing she was grinning like a kid.

"How was it?" he asked.

"Looks like I'm buying dinner," she said.

Rider ran a hand through his hair wearily. It wasn't that anything was really going wrong. In fact, the most important things were progressing right on schedule. It was the little things that were not quite coming together and driving him nuts.

The best thing he could say was that it wasn't because of any of the Redstone people: it was people on the outside who were falling down on the job. The man who was supposed to have run the final test on the air-conditioning system had been delayed. And two important shipments of extra bedsheets—Redstone Resorts always triple sheeted the beds, so no blanket ever touched a guest's skin—and the last of the gym equipment were held up in Arethusa, something about a bomb scare. He made a note to put that in his next report to Redstone. If the unrest kept escalating, they might have to make other arrangements.

He glanced at his watch as he'd been doing all afternoon. Still plenty of time before dinner. His mouth twisted wryly; he was acting like a teenager with a hot date. But he couldn't deny he was eager—and apprehensive—about dinner with Paige tonight. They'd kept it light, under the guise of a bet being paid off, but he knew she could have gotten out of it if she'd wanted to, since she'd never actually agreed to that part of it.

But she hadn't. And he wasn't sure why. Was she only trying to show him she was keeping to their agreement? Or did she want to—

"Mr. Rider?"

He glanced up to find Elan Kiskeya, the young man they'd decided to give a shot at replacing Bohio, in his doorway.

"Come on in," he said, glad enough of the interruption.

"I won't keep you," the young man said. "I just wanted to tell you the elevator system is ready for you to check."

"Already?" Rider asked, surprised.

"Yes, sir." Kiskeya's voice was full of pride. And rightfully so, Rider thought.

"Good job, Elan. I figured we were a couple of days away on that."

"Thank you. And thank you again for taking a chance on me."

"No...thank you," Rider answered. "You're making me look good. I'll be sure they hear about you at Redstone."

"Thank you. I already enjoy working for them."

He liked it when a gamble paid off, Rider thought as the young man hastened away, off to work even harder, he guessed. When Josh had first given him the power to make field promotions, he'd been wary; personnel wasn't his field. But he'd been right more than he'd been wrong, and that was all Josh asked.

In a way, Rider thought, he was in a unique position to understand the vast scope of Josh's vision. He'd come directly from an earthquake-ravaged part of the Middle East, where Redstone was helping finance a massive rebuilding effort, to this place catering to the movers and shakers. He found it to be an education in itself. And after nearly fifteen years Rider was as impressed as he had been in the beginning.

He decided abruptly that three hours in this office dealing with paperwork and details was enough for today, and got to his feet. He needed to check the generator tests, and then he'd stop by and sign off on Kiskeya's work. By then Barry would be waiting—and probably fussing—to start the final check on the rooms in the north building, and after that he'd head back. He'd already told Rudy to fire up the grill for his special meal.

By the time he finished, including some reinforcement

of his appreciation for Kiskeya's good job, he was running late. He took the shortcut back to the main building where his room was, cutting through the garden.

He froze in front of a hibiscus bush when some leaves rustled off to his left. A much more definite rustle than just the current slight breeze. In a burst of idiocy his brain ran through the list of creatures native to the island—iguanas, the odd but harmless mastiff bat, tiger beetles—even though he already knew none of them were particularly threatening to humans.

He held his breath and listened with a hunter's ears. The old, long-unused skills came back surprisingly well. Something large, and tall, the sounds were coming from at least a couple of feet above the ground. Only one thing fitted that description on the island. And then the breeze shifted slightly, he caught the smell of cigarette smoke, and he knew he was right.

He turned and took a careful step, then another, moving silently, in the old stalking way, past the hibiscus and into the tropical grass that was the flowering bush's backdrop. There he found his quarry; a boy crouched hiding in the thicket of tall grasses, smoking a cigarette.

Or trying to; the face he was making and the sudden burst of smothered coughing told Rider he hadn't been at it long.

"Get rid of the butt of that cancer stick somewhere else," he said.

The boy let out a strangled yelp and scrambled to his feet. His baseball cap fell backward off his head. The sunglasses he wore slipped to the end of his nose. The cigarette dropped onto his shirt, and he swatted it wildly. It hit the ground, glowing orange. The boy instinctively moved his foot to crush it out, but stopped abruptly, apparently remembering shoes hadn't been in his wardrobe today.

Rider stepped on the cigarette, but didn't grind it. He picked it up, and handed it back to the boy.

"Tell me you didn't get that here."

"Huh?"

Rider tried again. "Where'd you get the cigarette?"

"Oh. I brought it from home."

"Good."

"Huh?"

"I didn't want to have to fire somebody."

The boy looked blank. "Fire somebody?"

"For selling them to an underage kid."

The boy stiffened. "I'm not a kid."

"Prove it. Be smart enough not to smoke."

"Yeah, yeah," the boy muttered in the tone of one who'd heard it all before. As perhaps he had. Then he gave Rider a sideways look. "You're Rider, aren't you? The big kahuna around here?"

"I'm Rider, at least," he agreed.

"I remember you."

Rider blinked. He hadn't met any of the children on the island yet, so how could—

It hit him then. "You're Kyle?"

The boy nodded. "I remember when you were there. When my dad died."

He said it levelly enough, but Rider could hear the lingering pain behind the words.

"That was a tough time."

"My mom said you made sure he got brought home."

"I did what I could."

The boy stood up straighter. "Thanks," he said, and held out his hand. Startled, Rider took it. While the boy's grip was firm, his palm was sweaty. But the gesture was very adult, and Rider treated it that way.

"You're welcome, Kyle. I wish I could have done more."

And in the next instant the boy was back. He plucked a leaf from the hibiscus, and nervously started to fold it into a tiny square. "You going to tell my mom? About me smoking?"

He had been only ten when his father had died, and when Rider had first seen him he'd been dazed by what had happened, not quite comprehending yet that death truly did mean forever. He'd changed a lot, of course, since then, but Rider could still see traces of the child in the teenager, although the sullen set of the mouth was new, as was the half-shaved head with the thick mop of slightly maroon hair above it, and the earrings piercing his left lobe.

"Well? You gonna tell her?"

"I'm not sure." He drew in a breath; the smell of smoke was fading now. "How much will it hurt her?"

The boy flinched but recovered quickly. "Probably none. She doesn't care what I do."

"Oh?" If there was one thing about Paige he was certain of, it was that this boy was her life.

"She doesn't care about me at all. If she did, she wouldn't have dragged me here, away from my friends."

"So why did she?"

"She *says* it was to keep me out of trouble. But I wasn't really in trouble, she just doesn't understand. She never does."

"At least she cared. Maybe you should be glad of that."

"Yeah, sure," the boy said sarcastically. "Look, she doesn't like my friends, doesn't like what I like to do, doesn't like my video games. She doesn't like anything!"

She liked flying, Rider thought, picturing her face this morning and the huge smile she'd given him when she'd landed.

"And now she's my teacher, too, and it really sucks."

"I can understand how that would be tough," Rider said neutrally.

"She just wants me to work and study all the time." Kyle added a four-letter word that succinctly pronounced his opinion of that.

"You know, swearing doesn't make you an adult any more than smoking does."

"Oh, yeah, and I guess you never swear?"

"Me? Oh, sure I do, when provoked. In fact, I can say what you just said in about nine different languages."

"Nine languages?" Kyle looked intrigued. Then he frowned. "So why are you on my case?"

"Swearing is best saved to make a point. If you use it all the time, it becomes meaningless."

"Huh?"

Rider smothered a sigh; he'd never realized talking to teenagers was so much work. "Look, if you wanted to...say, scare somebody with a firecracker. You set one off and they jump. You set off a whole string, they jump at the first one, but by the end of the string they're used to it and it doesn't scare them anymore."

"Oh."

Kyle said nothing more, but at least he looked thoughtful. Rider glanced at his watch and winced. He wondered if the boy knew he was going to be having dinner with his mother in less than ten minutes. He started walking again, and to his surprise the boy followed.

"Have you seen your mother this afternoon?" he asked.

"Nah. I try to avoid her." Kyle grimaced. "She's probably hunting for me for dinner by now, though. If I don't go back she'll be really snarly."

"Actually, maybe not," Rider told him. "She and I are having dinner at the restaurant in just a few minutes. Chef Aubert is using us as guinea pigs for something new."

The boy looked startled, then shrugged. "Rudy's cool. He's been just about everywhere in the world."

"I know. I ate at his restaurant in London, and then in Rome. After that I went on a campaign to get him for Redstone."

"You've been to London? And Rome?"

Rider nodded. "And just about every place in between."

"Wow." The boy was genuinely impressed now. "My dad used to travel a lot."

"I know." He said it carefully, not wanting to open up a subject he had no desire to get into.

"Once he brought me back something, too. A model of the Eiffel Tower, from Paris."

Odd, Rider thought. The boy spoke as if he'd had the perfect father, with nothing but love and sadness at his loss in his young voice. As if it didn't matter why his father had been on that plane when he died.

And you'd think a traveling father would bring something back for his only son more than once.

On impulse he said, "You're welcome to join us for dinner, if you want. You have to eat, anyway, and Rudy always has some good stories to tell when he's got a captive audience."

The boy hesitated, and suddenly Rider was anxious for him to come. "Of course, it'll be kind of adult discussion, so if you'll be bored..."

"I won't," Kyle said instantly, as Rider had thought he might.

And so he had company when he walked into what would be the main restaurant at the resort. Rudy had only been expecting the two of them, but a single extra body, even with a teenage boy's appetite, was but a minor obstacle for someone with Rudy's experience.

Paige was already seated at the table when they arrived. She was toying with her silverware, as if too nervous to simply sit still. Rider noticed she had a stack of folders on the seat beside her. They looked like the same ones she'd had at the meeting the day he'd arrived.

"I invited a friend," he said as they got to the table. She looked up quickly, apparently so intent on the fork that she hadn't realized they were there. "Hope you don't mind."

"No, of course not..."

Her voice trailed away and her eyes widened when she saw her son beside him. "Kyle?"

"He invited me," he said almost angrily, his chin jutting out slightly.

Rider wondered if Kyle remembered that they hadn't really settled the question of whether he would tell Paige he'd caught her son sneaking a smoke. If he did, it didn't show in his attitude, and Rider suddenly wondered why on earth he'd done this, invited the kid. He was clearly furious with his mother, and Rider doubted he himself would be able to stay out of it if Kyle continued to talk to her in that tone.

"Then sit down," was all Paige said.

Kyle did, glancing at the folders on the chair. He rolled his eyes. "You even brought school stuff here?"

To Rider's surprise, Paige blushed. "I thought Mr. Rider might want to see how things are going."

Rider was puzzled as he took a seat across from her, and then it struck him. The school papers were protection, so she could make this seem like a business dinner, not a personal one. He felt oddly disappointed by the realization.

It wasn't until Rudy arrived and muttered something in his ear about bringing your own buffer, that he realized he'd done the same thing. Inviting Kyle hadn't been for the boy's sake, it had been for his. Nothing could get too personal with Paige's fifteen-year-old son at the table with them.

He almost laughed aloud at the absurdity of it, both of them so busy protecting themselves from the possibilities.

He wondered if that meant she was as tempted by them as he was.

Paige got over her nervousness rather quickly, if only because she was wondering who this kid was sitting at the table. The sullen, snippy teenager she'd almost grown used to was nowhere in sight. This Kyle wasn't the outgoing, friendly boy he'd once been, but he was considerably more civil and sociable than he'd been with her for longer than she cared to remember.

He seemed more than willing to talk to Noah, and listened to what he said with every appearance of rapt interest. When their food came, he even ate like a normal person, instead of shoveling it in as fast as he could in order to escape. And when Rudy sat down for a few minutes, to get their reviews of his experiment—fresh mahi grilled with his personal choice of spices that had given it a wild combination of flavors that somehow worked—Kyle was downright friendly to him, as well.

Paige was aware she wasn't sharing in the conversation very much, but it had been so long since she'd seen her son act like a human being she didn't want to waste it. Even though she realized that to Noah he probably seemed like a normal, even likable kid.

Eventually Kyle asked Noah what time it was, and when he said nearly eight, the boy stood up.

"I gotta go. Thanks, Mr. Rider."

More courtesy than I get, Paige thought. She was curious about where he was going, but knew if she asked she would only get that pained look he did so well, accusing her of treating him like a child.

"Be home by ten. School tomorrow."

He glared at her. "This isn't—" He stopped himself, as if aware that what he was going to say—This isn't my home—might insult his new friend. "Later," he muttered, and left.

Paige smothered a sigh.

"How long has the attitude been going on?"

Paige looked at him in surprise. "I thought he was perfectly nice to you."

"He was. It was you he was treating like a pariah. When he bothered to acknowledge you exist at all."

She was surprised again—this time that he'd noticed and had bothered to mention it.

She tried to shrug as if it didn't matter. It did. And she knew there would come a time when she was going to have to start demanding respect from Kyle. But tonight had made it clear that that time was here and now. She didn't like being humiliated ever, but in front of this man it was unbearable.

"He's still hurting," she said. "I know it's been five years, but they're very tough years for a boy."

For a long moment the silence spun out. Noah seemed about to speak twice, but stopped. Then finally, slowly, words began to come.

"After my mom was killed in a car accident when I was Kyle's age, my dad came down on me hard. He was tough on my sister, Michelle, too, but he really caged me. Stopped me from doing everything but going to school."

Paige frowned. "That must have been hard."

"It was. We'd always been close, hunting, fishing together, that kind of thing, so it hurt."

"He even stopped that? Why?"

"For a long time, I didn't know. I heard people tell him he should cut me some slack, I'd just lost my mother. He ignored them."

That one hit close to home; she'd been giving Kyle slack for five years, and look where it had gotten her.

"Finally one day, when I wanted to get my driver's license and he wouldn't let me, we had a huge fight. I yelled at him, he yelled back at me, it escalated, and I...put my fist through a wall." He flexed his right hand as if at the memory.

"And is that when you found out?"

He let out a compressed breath, as if for that moment he truly had been back in that painful time.

"Yeah. He finally said something that made sense out of it. I realized he was scared to death of losing me, too, and the only way he could think of to keep that from happening was to keep me where he could look out for me.

Michelle was less trouble, she was younger and still home most of the time, anyway. But he wanted me in sight all the time. If I wasn't, he got scared.''

Paige felt the sting of moisture in her eyes. "I know the feeling," she said, her voice tight. "I wanted to do the same thing with Kyle."

"I guess my point is...once I understood that, I didn't mind so much. In a way it was my dad showing me how much he loved me."

If she'd needed any encouragement to do what she'd been putting off, it had just been given to her. "Thank you," she said. "That helps me...know what to do."

Noah shrugged then, leaning back, looking at his glass, his empty plate, anywhere but at her face, as if he was now sorry he'd opened up quite that much.

"Did you and your dad make up?" she asked.

He nodded. "We're fine now. I get back to see him two or three times a year." Given his traveling schedule, Paige guessed that was more difficult than he made it sound. "He does most of his hunting with a camera now, but we still head out into the backcountry at least once a year."

"Did he ever...remarry?"

"Not yet." Noah grinned. "But there's a woman down the street who's got her eye on him, and she's a pretty smart lady. I may get a stepmother yet."

Paige smiled, took a sip of the excellent wine Rudy had recommended, then stopped with the glass still to her lips when Noah asked, "What about you?"

"Me?"

"You haven't remarried."

"No."

"Must be some likely candidates."

"No."

"I find that hard to believe. Are the guys in L.A. blind or just stupid?"

She told herself it was the alcohol causing her flush, but

she knew better. "Maybe I'm just not in the market to get married again. What about you?" she asked, hoping to divert the conversation.

For a moment he looked as if he were sorry he'd started this, but he did answer. "Married once and almost a second time. Both of them bailed for the same reason."

"Your work?" Paige guessed.

His mouth quirked. "Am I wearing a sign? Something only women can see?"

"Maybe only women worry about whether the man in their life will put them first or not."

"I do remember the phrase *second fiddle* being tossed around." His tone was wry, but Paige sensed there was genuine regret behind the words.

Paige grimaced. "I would have settled for second. Fourth or fifth was a little tougher to take."

Noah's gaze fastened on her, his eyes full of some emotion she wasn't sure she could name, and she had the oddest feeling that he knew more than he could possibly have guessed about her marriage.

"You should never have to settle," he said.

The intensity of his look rattled her, as if they had turned some corner she'd known was there but hadn't expected to reach just yet.

"Doesn't everyone settle in one way or another?" She said it lightly, trying to move this back to safer ground.

"It shouldn't be that way," he said flatly. "I understand now why Carrie left, and Linda practically ran from the altar."

A vivid image of Noah Rider waiting at a flower-bedecked church for a woman he loved enough to ask to marry him flashed through her mind. And for that instant none of the reasons she'd believed so strongly for so long seemed important enough that she would run. Not if he was the one waiting for her.

Chapter 5

She'd known. He'd tried to get there before she heard on the radio or saw it on TV, but he'd been too late. The woman who'd answered the door when he rang the bell had that hollow-eyed look people got when death has struck close.

He'd only had to do this a couple of times—Josh spread it out so that nobody got the unpleasant duty too often— but that didn't make it any easier.

"Mrs. Cooper, I'm Noah Rider, from Redstone. We met last year, briefly. I'm here to help," he'd said. The standard, simple opening, a truth that did nothing to change what had happened or what was to come.

Rider awoke with a start. It had been a long time since he'd had that dream. But this time was no different from all the others—the memories flooded him. That night was so vividly etched in his mind. He remembered thinking about the last time he'd seen her, at the dinner given when the deal between her husband's company and Redstone had been finalized. That woman, dressed sleekly in a deep-blue gown that had turned her red hair to fire, bore little resemblance to the woman who had opened the door of the home whose family had just been forever changed.

He'd been seated next to her at dinner that night, and he'd thought she was lovely. They'd talked, and he'd found he was enjoying himself more than he ever did at those things, even laughing out loud more than once at her easy wit.

And then he'd been given this awful job, simply because he'd had the misfortune to be in Portugal three weeks before Flight 78 went down.

He'd handled the calls, both incoming and outgoing, so she didn't have to go through it over and over. He'd fought through the red tape of bringing Phil home from a foreign country. He'd handled every detail, down to providing catered food for the inevitable stream of visitors offering condolences. He'd helped wherever he could, including with the heartbroken Kyle.

And when she'd finally broken down late one night, he'd held her. He'd let her cry, she'd thanked him, and pulled herself together with a strength that made a mockery of the idea of women as the weaker sex.

She'd gotten through the funeral, and the gathering after, with that same strength. But early that evening, as he'd been preparing to leave, his job finished, something changed. He didn't know what, but thought it might be some kind of post-traumatic stress. She'd had a fight with Kyle earlier, the boy had stomped out of the house to a friend's, and he was worried about her being alone. She seemed dazed at first, then wobbled back and forth between anger and tears. He supposed it was part of the natural process, and wondered if he should stay.

He had tried to ask her. When she whispered, "Stay," he thought she'd wanted his shoulder again. But she'd made it clear in the next few minutes that she wanted much, much more.

As vividly as if it had just happened he remembered the heat of her kiss, remembered the hot, surging response of his body, remembered the soft, luscious feel of her clinging to him, remembered the feel of her breast against his palm. She'd begun it, and he'd lost all sight of reality in the fire she kindled. Only the noise Kyle made, returning unexpectedly, snapped him out of it. And only then did it really hit home what he was doing.

And the image of himself, his hands roving over her body, his mouth dancing against hers, of himself allowing that to happen, had haunted him ever since. It had both taunted him and berated him, adding to his utter confusion; up until that night, he'd been seriously considering trying to mend the breach with Linda. The only thing that saved him was the thought that he'd likely never see Paige again.

And now here he was.

He sat up, rubbing at his eyes. He'd left the slider open, and the night breeze brought him the scent of the sweet, warm tropical air. He tossed off the sheet that was all he needed in this balmy locale, and stood up. He didn't bother to dress—it was night and he wasn't going to go beyond his own lanai, which was in shadow anyway.

He stood there in those shadows, letting the breeze wash over him.

All he had to do was get through ten days. He should be glad he'd had the chance to apologize and that she'd not only accepted it but had insisted on lifting some of the blame from him. That should have changed everything, should have freed him from the dream.

It hadn't. He was glad, but it hadn't helped a bit.

She had tried to start this reasonably, to talk to Kyle in a sane, courteous manner. But when she broached the subject in the morning at their small kitchen table, he shut down immediately.

"I hate you for bringing me here. I'll always hate you."

All right, she thought. If he truly hated her for removing him from all that—including his precious video games— then so be it. Even if it meant she sometimes felt even more alone than she had after Phil's plane had gone down, leaving her with a ten-year-old boy, no job and the devastating knowledge that they were nearly broke because the husband who had promised he would take care of everything had in fact taken care of nothing. If it hadn't been for Joshua Redstone...

She drew in a deep breath. She stood up, needing the tiny extra edge of looking down at him.

"All right. You hate me. That's a distinct change in our relationship, and therefore the rules will now change."

She saw the word *rules* had caught his attention, but he still refused to look at her.

"Obviously it's impossible for you to be pleasant to me, but as of now you will no longer show me disrespect. You don't have to love me or even like me, but you will show me the same courtesy you show any other adult."

"That's—"

"Be quiet."

Kyle blinked, startled.

"You will do your schoolwork without protest and on time. If it is not done, you will remain after school until it is. You now have half an hour to socialize after school, then you will be home until your homework is completed. If you leave the house after that you will either tell me or leave a note about where you're going, with whom and when you'll be back. If you want to go somewhere outside of the resort itself, you will ask permission first, and you will tell me where you're going and who you will be with and when you'll be back. And you will do it without being rude and without dramatics."

Kyle stared, his eyes widening. "That's not fair!"

"Neither is how you've been treating me. Now, the consequences of violating these rules will be immediate. First,

you will return here and complete the work you've not
done, or think about what you have done that landed you
here—for the remainder of that day. And for the next week
you will be limited to the grounds of the resort, not including the beach.''

"But—"

"Quiet. You have no say in this. A second violation will
result in grounding to this bungalow until I say different.
Got that?''

Kyle scrambled to his feet. She could see he was ready
to bolt.

"And if you run away now, you will be very, very sorry.
I am legally in charge of you for three more years. If you
would like to see how awful I can make them for you, just
keep pushing.''

Slowly, gaping in shocked disbelief, Kyle sank back
down into his chair.

"One last thing,'' she said. "You say you hate me. Fine,
that's your choice. But know this. Somehow, some way,
you're going to become the best person you can be, no
matter what I have to do.''

She leaned forward, hands on the table, and it was a
measure of Kyle's stunned state that he didn't pull back
from her.

"And remember this. I love you. And nothing you can
ever do will change that. I will never, *ever* give up on you.''

Shell-shocked was the phrase that came to Paige's mind.
He looked shell-shocked. Deciding her point was made, she
headed back to her room to gather up papers for the school
day and left him there.

He never looked at her the entire day in school, but Paige
was grateful he'd shown up at all. He left the moment class
was over, and she saw he was headed for the bungalow.
She purposely didn't hurry. She'd laid down the rules, it
was up to him now. It had hurt her to do it, more than Kyle
would ever know, but they simply couldn't go on the way

they had been. He'd been headed nowhere good, and it had to be stopped.

And Noah had given her the strength to do it. The strength and the direction. She didn't know if he'd intended to, but she did sense it wasn't like him to pour out his past to a near stranger like that.

Even if it was a stranger he'd once kissed like a long-lost lover.

She shivered inwardly at the memory that never seemed to lose any of its power, no matter how long it had been or how much she tried to stifle it.

"Are you all right, Mrs. Cooper?"

She looked up to see Lani DeSouza standing before her. "I'm fine, Lani. What did you need?"

"I wanted to give you my extra-credit history paper."

Paige smiled as she took the pages from the girl. "I'm going to have to invent something higher than an A-plus for you."

Lani giggled. "I love the way you teach it, especially when you translate it into modern speech."

It was one of her favorite things to do, to translate what was usually a stuffy or dry historical event into modern-day terms; it seemed to get through to the kids in a way nothing else did.

Lani, she thought as the girl left, was a beautiful girl now; as a woman she would be beyond stunning. Paige finished gathering her papers and headed out of the now empty schoolhouse. But she stopped in the doorway when she heard Kyle's voice. She couldn't tell what he'd said, but Lani's voice was quite clear.

"You Americans, you think you're better then everybody."

Kyle said something else she still couldn't hear.

"No, you're not bad, you're just like…like a big puppy, good in your heart but clumsy, and sometimes hurting people when you don't mean to."

She wished she could have heard what had started *that* conversation, Paige thought. Perhaps Kyle had again let slip his opinion of Lani's home. She'd heard the girl once telling him he was foolish for preferring "silly video games" to a good life here on her island. It made her glad she'd made him leave the video games behind.

The voices got fainter as the two moved away and she headed back to the bungalow. But once she'd arrived and changed clothes, she felt too restless to stay there. She grabbed her wide-brimmed hat and started out on a walk, choosing a direction she'd not taken before, up the slope away from the resort. The path wasn't as well delineated as the ones on the resort grounds, but it was clear enough as it wound through the trees and bushes. She saw the occasional lizard and several darting crested hummingbirds. And every few feet she caught a glimpse of the water, each time from a different angle.

At the top of the slope the path became more difficult and overgrown than she wanted to tackle, and she needed to see that Kyle was following the new rules, so she turned to go back. Something caught her eye out in the water, and she leaned forward to look. Three small boats sat in the distance, one of them larger than the other two. It wasn't unusual to see a boat out there, but she'd never seen three together before. The larger one appeared to be a fishing boat, and she wondered what they were catching. Marlin, perhaps? That's what she always thought of, films of the huge, graceful fish leaping its length and more out of aquamarine water. But for all she knew, they didn't even live around here.

She should send for some books on the local wildlife and plant life, she thought as she headed back. It would be good for her own sake to know, and also in case the kids who weren't native to the island wanted to know. She'd go online tonight and see what was available.

She was lost in thought as she walked back across the

resort courtyard, until for the second time she heard Kyle's voice. Snapping back to herself, she looked around and saw him sitting on a bench with his back to her. Next to him sat Noah.

Another conversation I'd love to hear, she thought. She wouldn't stoop to eavesdropping, but there was, she decided, no reason she couldn't just keep walking as she had been. So she did, and as she got closer she began to hear bits and pieces.

"—go places, like my dad," Kyle was saying. "I'm not going to be afraid to go anywhere, like my mother."

Paige winced, but Noah pointed out reasonably, "She came here."

She didn't hear what Kyle said then, and it was probably just as well.

"Did you ever stop to think that maybe she didn't want to leave, either? That she gave up her own life for your sake?"

She wanted to hug him for his support.

Kyle snorted. "Yeah, right." Brushing off the possibility he asked, "So, when you were in Egypt, did you see the pyramids? And the sphinx?"

Noah grinned. "I don't think they let you out of the country until you do."

"Someday I'm going to see them. I'm going to see everything, as soon as I get out of school. And my mom can't stop me. I'm going around the world, just like my dad!"

Paige felt something cramp up inside her. For years she'd fought through the shambles of the life left her by her globe-trotting husband, and now here was her son wanting to do the same thing. She didn't think she'd made a sound, but Noah looked up. When he did, so did Kyle, and the boy's exuberance vanished.

"I suppose you came to tell me I'm late and in violation?" he said with a sneer.

She sensed Noah stiffen, but didn't look at him. She

glanced at her watch and said, her voice as calm as she could manage, "Actually, you have three minutes left. However, since you've just been extremely rude, yes, you're in violation. You'll go home and stay there until school tomorrow."

Kyle turned to Noah, disbelief clear in his face. "Can you believe that?"

"I can," Noah said, his voice cold. "If I'd ever spoken to my mother in that tone of voice, I'd have been grounded until I was forty. And I probably wouldn't have been able to sit for most of it."

Looking as if an idol had betrayed him, Kyle threw a last angry glare at Paige and then took off toward the bungalow at a run. Once he was out of sight, Paige sank down onto the bench, her knees a little wobbly after this first test of the new management.

"Thanks," she said after a moment.

"I gather you laid down the law?"

She nodded. "And as you can see, it didn't go particularly well."

"He'll come around. He's not a bad kid, he's just a little screwed up right now."

"I hope so." Her mouth twisted. "But I don't like hearing him talk about taking off like that."

"It's natural for a kid to want to see the world."

"Globe-trotting," she said grimly.

"We don't all have horns and a pitchfork," he said mildly.

Embarrassed, Paige quickly apologized. "I'm sorry. I'm just a little touchy. Having your son declare he hates you and always will at every opportunity isn't the easiest thing to live with."

"I imagine not." He looked at her consideringly for a moment. Then very evenly he said, "He seems to still have a great love for his father."

Paige sighed. "Yes, he does."

"You don't sound particularly happy about that."

Paige looked at him then, seeing in his eyes the same gentle warmth that had been there the night he'd shown up on her doorstep. And suddenly the past was alive and beating at her, as strong as it had been the day of Phil's funeral, when the farce had been revealed.

"Paige?"

She didn't know what must have shown in her face. She only knew she had to let out the emotion that was boiling up inside.

"I'm sorry," she said again, "but Phil's endless traveling was a real sore spot. We argued about it constantly."

She half expected him to defend Phil. He was a globe-trotter himself, after all. But he said nothing. After a moment she went on.

"It wasn't even the frequency, it was that he never made an effort to come home in between. If he had less than two weeks between jaunts, he just stayed away. Kyle really didn't know his father at all."

Noah shook his head. "Shouldn't be that way. You have a kid, you make some changes."

She gave him a sideways look. "Would you have made changes?"

He didn't toss off a glib answer, which she appreciated. After a moment he said, "Yes. There are ways to work around it. No matter if you're in the Aviation Division, or Tech, or resorts, Redstone's always willing to schedule so you have time to come home in between trips. It's tougher, but it can be done."

"Not according to Phil. The only thing he did was be gone more."

"Did you ever travel with him? Before Kyle?"

"No. I was working then, and I couldn't get away for those lengths of time." Her mouth twisted. "Besides, he never asked."

"His loss," Noah said softly.

Something in his tone broke the barrier she'd managed to keep in place until now. The words, words she'd never spoken to anyone, came out in a rush.

"He didn't think so. And when he got on that plane that last time? He had no intention of ever coming back."

Noah went very still. She kept going, needing to share this with somebody, needing to vent the pain she'd kept bottled up for five years. At the same time, she couldn't quite believe she was telling him what she had told no one, speaking the words she had never, ever said to another human being.

"He had finally decided he no longer wanted either of us. He didn't want to be my husband and certainly not a father. He wanted his complete freedom, and he was leaving the country to be sure he got it."

"Paige—"

"You know how I found out?"

Her voice was sharp, abrupt, but she couldn't help it. She'd spent five years being grateful no one else knew, five years telling herself that at least her humiliation was private, that Phil had died before it became known that he didn't love her or even his son enough to stay, and now she was blurting it out to this man, of all people.

"Go ahead," Noah said, not really answering her question but sounding as if her pain was somehow stabbing at him.

"I got served with divorce papers. Certified mail, delivered the day of his funeral, can you believe that?" He visibly winced. "Lovely, huh? And with them was a letter saying he'd left us the house and would provide child support for Kyle from a trust he'd set up, but we were never to try and find him. That he never wanted to see me, or even his son, again."

"Paige, he was an idiot."

"No, he was cruel," she countered. "Why else would he spend a page of that letter telling me about the wonderful new woman he'd found in London, how much smarter, prettier and more sophisticated she was than me, and how he couldn't wait to be free to start his new life with her? Me, I was so pitiful I went back through his records to try to find out how long it had been going on.''

''Did it matter?''

She met his gaze then, aware of something niggling away at the edge of her consciousness, but not sure what it was. She answered him. ''To me it did. At least, it did then. Later I started wondering if she was the only one, if there had been more. A girl in every port, as they say.''

''What was the use?''

''Maybe I wanted to know just how big a fool I'd been.''

''Because you trusted? Because you expected the man you'd married to be honest, and worthy of that trust? You had a right to that expectation, Paige. It wasn't your fault he couldn't live up to it.''

''According to Phil it was.''

''Some men just don't deserve a woman like you, or a family. Phil was one of them.''

There it was again, something she should be noticing, something she should see.

''You know what's really crazy? After I found out, after I got over the first hurt, I wondered about her.'' She shook her head. ''Can you believe I actually felt bad for her?''

''Yes,'' Noah said, his voice so soft she could barely hear him. ''I can believe that of you.''

''I wondered if she was sitting alone somewhere, waiting for this man who'd promised to leave his wife for her. Maybe she even thought he was just one of those married men who always made the promise but never kept it. Maybe she never knew he was really coming for her.''

''She knew.''

''You think so? Do you think she was waiting at the airport for him, for the plane that would never come?''

''No.''

He was sounding hoarse now, as if each word was being ripped out of him.

"Noah?"

"She knew," he said in that awful voice, "because she was on that plane with him."

Paige stared at him. She opened her mouth to say "What?" but the word never came out. It hit her then, with the force of a blow, what had been bothering her during her outpouring. There had been many things in Noah's eyes: sympathy, support, reassurance, even anger.

What there hadn't been was surprise.

She couldn't seem to breathe. She also couldn't deny what was now so clear. His last words proved it.

He knew. He'd sat here listening to her sad story, her pitiful secret, and the whole time he'd already known.

Chapter 6

"Paige—"

"You knew," she said, her eyes wide with shock as she stared at him.

Rider shifted uncomfortably. "Yes."

"You knew about the woman, about the divorce? Both?"

"It came out during the Redstone post-crash investigation," he said, hating the way she was looking at him, as if he'd just shattered her world all over again. "And he had copies of the papers in his desk. We found them three days after the crash."

She went even paler, so pale he thought she might faint, and he wondered what he'd said now. But Paige didn't faint. She simply sat there, reminding him too painfully of how she had looked the first time he'd gone to her house after Redstone had confirmed her husband had been on that plane.

"We? You mean all of Redstone knew? And—" she

stopped for a gasping breath ''—you all knew even before
I did?''

He realized then what he'd done. The funeral, the day
she said she'd gotten the papers, had been five days after
the crash. ''Paige, I'm sorry—''

''Sorry?''

She leaped to her feet. She swayed slightly, but steadied
herself before he could reach out to do it. He stood up
slowly, wishing now he'd just kept his mouth shut. But the
image of her, freshly widowed and newly betrayed, still
having the compassion to worry about the other woman,
had been too much for him.

''You're sorry? You knew, days before, and you didn't
warn me? That I was about to be served divorce papers
from beyond the grave?''

''We tried to stop it altogether. Or at least delay it on
the grounds of changed circumstances.'' He rubbed at his
eyes; the tropical sun suddenly seemed painfully bright.
''But his lawyer was out of town, and by the time we
tracked him down, it was too late. They'd already been
sent.''

When he looked at her again, there was no doubting that
the betrayal shadowing her eyes this time was aimed at him.
''Why didn't you tell me? You were supposedly there to
help.''

''I didn't know. I didn't find out they'd already been sent
until I checked with the office that night. I didn't realize
you'd gotten the papers that day, or…I never would have
left you alone to deal with it. I was planning to delay my
trip and stay until they did arrive, but then…''

He let his voice trail off and saw by the tightening of
her lips that she realized what had changed his plans.

''It was all just rotten timing, that's all,'' he said, rubbing
at the back of his neck where a nasty tightness had settled
in.

A flicker of realization showed in her face. ''That's why

somebody from Redstone kept calling, and checking on me, after you left, isn't it? Because they knew."

He nodded. "I had to be in Tokyo, so they followed up."

"You could have told me. You knew about the papers— you could have at least told me that much."

"I was hoping they could stop it, that you'd never have to know at all."

She shivered visibly. "All this time I thought my humiliation was at least private. And now…"

"Paige, everybody at Redstone felt awful about the whole situation. And most of them were really mad at Phil."

"And you, what did you feel? Sympathy? Pity?"

He reached out and put a hand on her arm. "Paige, please, don't do this. You have no reason to feel humiliated."

She yanked free of him and stood there trembling. "You don't get it, do you? I have every reason to feel humiliated! Because if I hadn't gotten those damned papers, on *that* day, do you think I'd have thrown myself at you like the proverbial love-starved widow?"

Rider gaped at her, suddenly realizing that she wasn't on the verge of tears, she was on the verge of exploding. With anger. "What?" he said, wondering if it sounded half as stupid as he felt just now.

"If it hadn't been for those papers, on that day, I never would have made such a fool of myself. I never would have taken your…help as something else." She stood there, her quickened breathing audible, the eyes he'd always thought so warm, icy now with rage. "You should have told me. You could have saved yourself the embarrassment of getting mauled, and me five years of sleepless nights."

She turned on her heel and walked away, each step rigid with a control that bit into him as deeply as her words had. He started after her, then stopped himself. He was probably the last person she wanted to see right now. And he wasn't sure he could blame her. He'd been trying to help, but it had well and truly backfired on him. And, more important, on Paige. So he stood there, feeling helpless and hating the feeling, staring after her.

A few minutes later he realized he was supposed to be in a meeting, and he snapped at Barry Rutherford's young assistant, who had hunted him down to remind him.

Great. What the hell else can go wrong? he muttered to himself as he turned and hurried toward the main building. And then, wary of the way things had been going today, he added, Don't answer that!

Paige shut the door behind her and leaned against it. She was gasping as if she'd run the length of the island and shivering as if that island were Iceland.

Kyle, thankfully, was shut in his room; she could see the door closed against her from here. She made her way to the lanai and dropped down into one of the lounges facing the water.

She hadn't thought it was possible for the situation around Phil's death to be any worse. Obviously, she'd been as big a fool about that as she had been about everything else.

Everything surrounding that time was now even uglier. She couldn't bear to wonder what Noah must have thought then. And now that she knew all of Redstone had known the truth, she wondered if he'd really been chosen to come because he'd just been in Portugal.

More likely, he got the short straw, she thought. And got jumped by the widow for his trouble.

In a convulsive movement she curled up on the lounge, drawing her knees up as if she could somehow save herself from damage already done. She felt the tears begin, fought them helplessly, uselessly. She hadn't allowed herself to cry for a very long time, but now she couldn't stop.

She wished she could just stay here, lock the door and

hide until Noah left the island. Never have to face him again. But she couldn't. She had children to teach, children she'd made a commitment to—including the stubborn boy in the next room—and she had to honor that commitment. And she would. The best she could do was try to avoid running into Noah.

She lay there, trying uselessly not to think for a long time. The tears slowed and finally stopped. Gradually her shaking stopped, as well, but the sick feeling in the pit of her stomach lingered on and on. She tried taking long, deep breaths, and it helped a little. And after a while her body began to return to normal. Her mind, however, continued to churn.

The breeze picked up, as it always did in the evenings. It brought her the scent of the flowers, frangipani and a variety of ginger, the head gardener had told her.

She'd been moved by all the flowers Redstone had sent to Phil's funeral. And by the Redstone people who had shown up. Now all she could think of was that they'd all known, all been there because they felt sorry for the poor, cheated-on wife. How many of them had known what Phil was doing? Had some of them even met the woman?

She shivered anew and wrapped her arms tighter around herself. Even Joshua Redstone had come, and the tall, lanky, unassuming man had graciously—and she would have sworn sincerely—offered his condolences and any help that he or his company could give her.

Maybe he hadn't known. Maybe it hadn't filtered up that far.

You're not that lucky, she told herself bitterly.

And then, spiking through her like an unexpected shaft of light, came the thought, But you're luckier than she was.

That cooled her anger a little. In those days, five years ago, she had been devastated by the discovery that the husband she had loved hadn't loved her at all. But the thought of the nameless and thankfully faceless woman who had literally died for Phil's brand of love gave her back a little perspective.

She sat up, wiping at her burning eyes. She retreated to her bedroom, where she tried to mask the ravages of her outburst as best she could. Not that Kyle would notice or care in his current mood, but she didn't want to have to explain. Or lie. There'd been enough lies. Too many lies.

She got through the next day fairly well, she thought. If Kyle noticed anything wrong, he didn't want to talk to her enough to find out what. Even when she told him he was released from the house—with the same rules in effect— he'd barely spoken.

She didn't see Noah, which helped. She wondered if he were avoiding her, too, considering rarely had a day gone by that she hadn't seen him at least two or three times. In fact, she only realized now a day hadn't gone by since he'd been here that they hadn't talked. Not just said hello in passing, but actually talked. She didn't realize until now how much she'd looked forward to those moments, even with all the baggage they had between them.

Which was nothing compared to the baggage between them now.

"You're whining," she said aloud that night when she felt tears threaten again. "What difference does it make if the whole world knew before you did? It doesn't change the facts."

That made her feel better, so she added, "And it wasn't Noah's fault. It was none of his business really, and you should be thankful he even tried."

That said, she turned out the light and got the first decent sleep she'd had in two days.

By the next morning she had her equilibrium and her composure back. She managed to be cheerful enough during the early session to annoy Kyle, who then stayed at school for lunch period. Although she suspected that the fact Lani was usually there, as well, had something to do with that.

She had to admit not dealing with her cranky son made her own lunch break much sunnier. She even left early to go back to the school, feeling like someone going outside for the first time after an illness; everything seemed a bit clearer, more vivid, in sharper focus.

She was startled when she glimpsed a young man in what looked like camouflage pants back in the trees above the resort, but guessed he must be an employee she hadn't met yet or a son of one of the locals. Even Kyle had a pair of those pants, but she was surprised the trend had spread this far.

Wondering if she would find Kyle and Lani in another esoteric discussion, she headed toward the schoolhouse.

Shoving his hands in the pockets of his khaki pants Rider leaned back against the wall of the pool house, where the recreation director was giving him the final inventory count on towels, chairs, bottles of suntan lotion and all the other equipment that came with the territory. He'd been paying attention, too. At least, he had been until he'd caught a glimpse of sunlight on coppery hair.

He watched Paige walk across the courtyard, heading, he guessed, for the schoolhouse. He'd made sure to be scarce yesterday, trying to give her the distance he guessed she needed since he'd so clumsily betrayed that her husband's desertion had been, if not common knowledge, then at least hardly a secret.

But it hadn't been easy. He'd had to fight the urge to go to her, to try and make her understand he'd never meant to hurt her or make things worse than they already were. He'd hated leaving that night. He'd meant it when he'd told her he had planned to dump his scheduled departure for Tokyo and stay until the divorce papers had arrived. He'd even had some idea about intercepting them. But he'd been tied up with the funeral arrangements most of the day, never guessing that of all days that would be the one when they arrived.

And then, after that unexpected, passionately hot embrace and kiss, she had virtually ordered him to leave. She'd been embarrassed, he knew, but until now he'd had no idea what else she'd been feeling.

…five years of sleepless nights.

In the midst of the emotional turmoil he took some small comfort in that. He'd thought himself alone in those restless nights.

A movement in the distant trees caught his eye. He straightened up, pulling off his sunglasses as he narrowed his eyes. It was a man, no one he'd seen before, and it took Rider a moment to figure out why he was so hard to see. And then, as the man headed in the same general direction Paige had, he stepped into a brighter spot among the trees. Rider saw that he was dressed in the traditional green camouflage, doing what it was supposed to in the thick greenery around the resort. He looked young and seemed to know where he was going.

Or he was following somebody who knew where they were going, he thought suddenly.

Paige?

He considered that as he pulled a pen out of the pocket of the Hawaiian shirt he'd resorted to again today—it had become clear to him why they were popular in tropical climes—and signed off on the clipboard the recreation director handed him. He considered the possibility that the man was here to meet her. The thought that she might be seeing someone here hadn't occurred to him. Besides, she'd told him there was no one.

His mouth twisted. Maybe she'd decided it was time. Maybe he'd somehow driven her to it with his own idiocy.

Maybe, he thought, he should quit dealing in maybes and just find out. He didn't like the fact that this guy seemed to be skulking through the trees, anyway. As Redstone's highest-ranking representative on-site, he should go find out what the guy was doing. It was his job, after all.

"Thanks, Mario," he said.

"We're all ready for the weekend, Mr. Rider. No problems here."

"I can see that. Good job."

The man turned to lock up. Rider checked his cell phone for messages, and when for once he found none, he headed up toward the trees. But the man in green was nowhere in sight now, and Rider wondered if he was just some local come to see the resort that had grown on this end of his island.

He pondered his next move for a moment, then started toward the schoolhouse. It couldn't hurt.

The little building, painted a traditional white, looked absolutely picturesque, he thought as he reached the clearing. There was still no sign of the man, but there were several children milling around outside, some playing, some finishing lunches they'd apparently brought with them. And there was Paige. She must have stopped to talk to someone—the man in the camouflage pants?—for she was just now going up the steps, amid cheerful waves from many of the children.

And off to one side Rider saw Paige's son, looking miserable. Things must still be strained between him and his mother, Rider thought. But then he saw that Kyle was intently, almost hungrily watching an exotically lovely young girl who was talking to another boy, and he realized there was more than just his home situation making the boy unhappy.

He stood watching for a moment, but then turned his attention to the schoolhouse. He'd worked on the plans, and Paige had told him how it had turned out, but he hadn't made it over there to see it yet in person. He did need to check it out, he told himself. It was on his list, waiting to be signed off. And besides, he was curious to see how the changes he'd made worked in actual use.

And it would be a chance to see if Paige was still furious at him.

He headed toward the stairs. A few of the kids he'd met already recognized him and waved, although not with the obvious affection they'd shown Paige. Kyle glanced his way, seemed surprised to see him there but didn't wave. He supposed the boy was still mad at him, too, for siding with his mother over his attitude.

He still didn't understand it. How could that kid be so downright nasty to his mother, who not only far from deserved it but was also the only parent he had left? How could he still glorify a father who had died in the act of abandoning him for life, who had cared so little for his own son that he hadn't even said goodbye?

It made no sense to him. He'd loved his mother dearly, but he still remembered how angry he'd been when she'd died, even knowing she certainly hadn't chosen to leave him. If she had instead done what Kyle's father had done, he doubted he ever would have forgiven her.

And Paige had clearly tried so hard to make it easier on the boy. She—

He stopped in his tracks.

She *had* tried hard to make it easier on her son. Of course she had; what else would a woman who was capable of feeling compassion for the woman who had broken up her marriage do? And a woman who could do that...

She hadn't told him.

Chapter 7

The minute the thought formed in his head, Rider knew it was the truth. Paige had never told her son the real truth behind his father's death. Had never told him they were being abandoned, deserted, tossed aside for something newer, flashier, less complicated. And so Kyle had developed this idealized image of a man who could never do anything to tarnish it. It was the only explanation for the way the boy still idolized his father.

And it would be like her to keep that knowledge buried in her, carrying the burden alone so that her son wouldn't have to. And there was a decent chance Kyle would never encounter anyone who would know, or even if they did, would ever tell him his father had had every intention of never seeing him again.

The depth and strength of that kind of love amazed him. He wasn't sure he—or any man—was capable of it. But then he realized he had living proof of a man who did, in his own way. His father. He'd brought Rider's mom home to die, and he'd nursed her, cared for her until the very end, never complaining, treasuring each minute with the woman he loved stolen from the grim reaper. And he himself had given the old man some tough times in those years after his mother's death, but his dad never gave up.

He wondered if he had that kind of strength in him somewhere. If that kind of thing could be hereditary. He could only hope.

He started moving again, taking the four steps to the raised porch two at a time. It was an old-fashioned, one-room schoolhouse, built the way many buildings in the tropics were—raised off the ground to let air circulate beneath and to help avoid water damage in case of storm surge. But it was completely modern, with the indoor plumbing he'd joked to Paige about and the computer center she had been so excited about. It even smelled new. He thought he caught a whiff of fresh paint as he came through the small vestibule where students apparently stowed backpacks and other gear not immediately needed.

He paused in the doorway to the big room itself, looking. It was oriented so the double doors were at the rear. The large space was loosely divided into a half-dozen sections—one the computer center on the raised platform in the front corner, another where he saw small mats rolled up on shelves, he guessed for the younger ones to take naps or have a quiet time during the day.

The rest of the sections, separated only by office cubicle-type walls festooned with pictures and artwork of various types, seemed to be divided by age levels. At the front of the room were several rows of chairs with half desktops, smaller ones in the front, enough for all the students to sit at one time. A good setup, he thought; Paige couldn't be everywhere, but with the low walls, she could see if a problem arose anywhere in the room.

Right now she was seated at the front of the room on a brightly-covered sofa. There was a large desk behind it, flanked by two tall filing cabinets. Behind the desk, sofa and file arrangement was the other way into and out of the school, a single, solid mahogany door. In front of Paige was a long, low table, and she had papers spread out over it, studying them intently.

Her hair today wasn't in the usual braid, but pulled back into a jaunty ponytail at the back of her head. It hung halfway down her back, giving him the answer to one of the things he'd always wondered about, how long that red mane would be if let loose.

Heat jolted through him, and he took a moment to fight it down before he actually stepped into the room. An odd sort of tension stayed with him, as if he were wondering if the teacher would throw him out of class.

He only took a couple of steps before he noticed the floor. He stopped, staring, bemused. Teak wood had been used, because of the threat of water from severe storms and the rare hurricane that hit this island. It was beautiful and one of the few woods that wasn't a termite attractant in this climate. But now it had been decorated. Five sets of whimsical, cartoonish bare footprints had been painted in a path from the back of the room up to where Paige sat. In red, blue, green, orange and black, they wound their way crookedly around the different sections, then split into four separate paths as they approached her sofa and desk.

He found himself smiling as he followed the chubby little feet through the room. But when he got to where they split, he stopped and looked up again.

She was watching him, her expression unreadable. She was dressed simply in a pair of navy-blue cotton slacks with a navy trimmed white blouse and a pair of white canvas shoes. He thought she'd never looked lovelier.

Forcing himself to stop staring at her, he gestured down at the floor. "I don't know which path to take."

She smiled then, and he felt a little of the tension leave him. And she seemed quite calm, even friendly as she explained. "Red is for if you're angry about something. Blue if you're sad, no reason required. Black is for excuses, good or bad. Orange is if you're sorry about something. Green is for good news to share.''

Well, that makes it easy, Rider thought. With a quirk of his mouth he stepped out along the orange path. When he got to the end, she was standing. Everything he'd planned to say escaped him, and he just stood there for a moment. As if the silence made her uncomfortable, she explained even further.

''I used the sofa to make this place seem like home rather than school, to make me more approachable to the little ones. And I painted those paths—in water-soluble paint, by the way—to make it clear that it was okay to talk about all those things,'' she said, and added with the slightest emphasis, ''and that I'm always willing to listen.''

He stood there for a moment, struggling for words. Finally he said simply, ''I'm sorry.''

There were so many other things he wanted to say, to explain, but right now that ''I'm sorry'' was all he could manage.

After a moment of silence Paige nodded.

''All right.'' When he said nothing more, she left it at that and asked if he wanted to look around. ''You should see how your work paid off.''

He followed her around the room, listening as she pointed out the ways she was using the changes he'd made in the plans, from the audio/visual corner to the small library to the computer center.

''It must be difficult, teaching all different ages.''

''It can be. And there will be times when I have to call in someone for things I'm not as versed in, for the older kids.''

''Then you get time off, I hope?''

She smiled. ''Maybe. Or I'll stay and hope I learn, too.''

That didn't surprise him, he thought. ''How about your personal quarters? Everything all right?''

She nodded. "Who could ask for more than the Redstone pay scale plus meals and lodging?"

"Sounds cushy," Rider agreed, then gestured at the room. "*Until* you think about being the only teacher for the whole range of students from kindergarten to high school."

She gave him a smile that seemed to be thanking him for understanding. It warmed him.

"It's working, though, even with the addition of the island's resident children."

"It must be rough having them all in the same room," he said as she showed him how she'd divided up the big space.

"It gets hectic sometimes," she admitted. "There's nothing to stop the noise between the groups. But kids have a great capacity for tuning out what they don't want to hear."

"Honed on their parents, no doubt," Rider said dryly.

She smiled, but the fact that it didn't quite reach her eyes warned him things were still not going well at home.

"Is Kyle still angry?"

"Very. But he's still sticking to the rules, so far. Of course, the silent treatment goes with it."

Rider gave her a sympathetic half smile. "Me, I fought. Loud, every time my dad tightened his hold. We raised the roof more than once. I'm surprised the neighbors didn't call the cops."

She smiled back. "By the way, I should thank you for what you did."

He blinked. "For what?"

"For sharing that story with me. I knew I had to do something about Kyle, before I lost all his respect, but I was afraid to. You showed me a different perspective, one that was just what I needed to help me decide."

"But he's still mad."

"Yes. But he's still obeying, however reluctantly. I haven't lost him completely."

Rider nodded in understanding. "I don't think that will ever happen."

"I hope you're right. But," she said with a shake of her head that sent the ponytail bouncing, "one of these days he's going to realize I don't really have any control over him. He's already bigger and taller than I am."

Rider shook his head in turn. "That's physical control. That means little. It's the emotional sway you hold that counts, and you'll never lose that. You're his mother, and however angry he may be with you now, he'll come around."

"I just have to live that long," she said wryly.

Rider hesitated, then decided he needed to know, although he wasn't sure why.

"You never told him, did you? About the divorce and why Phil was on that plane?"

Her head snapped around to face him as she faltered midstride, then stopped where she was.

"How did you know that?"

"It's the only thing that makes sense. The only explanation for why he so obviously still loves and misses his dad, under the circumstances."

"Oh." She seemed somehow relieved by his answer.

"Why?" he asked.

"Why? What earthly good would it have done?"

"It might have made things easier on you."

"At the cost of destroying my son? What was I supposed to do, let a ten-year-old child help me carry my burden? He was already the only reason I went on, it would have been hideously unfair to ask that of him, too."

He wondered if she knew how incredible she was. He doubted it; she'd probably laugh at him if he told her so.

"He tried so hard to win his father's approval," she said. "No matter how much Phil ignored Kyle, that boy never gave up trying. How could I tell him it never would have happened no matter how long his father had lived?''

''Maybe,'' Rider said slowly, ''maybe someday he'll *need* to know that it never would have happened. That he didn't fall short, because no amount of time would have made a difference. He didn't fail, because there had never been any chance of succeeding. Maybe he'll need that to finally let go.''

He could tell by her expression that she'd never thought of it that way before. He hoped she would think about it, because he knew the strain between her and her son was wearing on her.

''Paige? Why did you marry him?''

Her mouth curled into a wry half smile. ''If you only know the hours I've spent trying to answer that. I guess because he talked a good game.''

''Salesman.''

She nodded. ''My parents had a very happy marriage, up until the day my father died. I thought I'd have that with Phil. He promised me I would, and fool that I was I believed him.''

''Maybe he meant it at the time,'' Rider said grudgingly.

''Maybe.'' She didn't sound convinced. But then, neither was he.

She continued showing him around, and he could see from the colorful, imaginative and in some cases very well-executed drawings that adorned the walls, and from glancing at the essays that were posted, that she was a teacher who got through to her students. Just as he would have suspected. He listened quietly, liking the pride he heard in her voice. He knew from the files that when Josh hired her she hadn't taught for several years, but she clearly had never lost her love for it.

''Is there anything else you need?''

''Need? No.''

He smiled at the careful way she phrased it. "Okay, want, then."

She smiled back then. "Other than having all the computers online instead of one, no."

"That's going to take more wiring than we could get done in time, but it's still on the list."

"Fine. We can make do with one for now."

Paige went on to discuss other school-related matters, and he lapsed into silence. By the time she'd finished, his mind was bursting with everything he wanted to say, to explain to her. Finally, guessing he had a limited amount of time before class started, he stopped at the foot of the barefoot trails.

"Can we go back up the orange path?"

She studied him for a moment, nodded, and led the way back to the sofa. He sat down beside her, trying to sort out where to begin. And then she surprised him by speaking first.

"Look, Noah, I'm sure you and everybody else at Redstone meant well. I only reacted as I did the other day out of remembered pain. I'm sorry, too. And I don't blame you for not telling me."

With those simple, honest and direct words she disarmed him completely. And as if her honesty were catching, he found himself blurting out the rest of the truth about that week choreographed in hell. He'd thought he would just never tell her, that there was no point, but now...he still wasn't sure there was a point, but he knew it had to come out.

"It wasn't just that I hoped you wouldn't ever have to know," he admitted. "I couldn't tell you. I couldn't tell you what a jerk he was when his body wasn't even home yet. Not when I was..."

"Was what?"

He let out a compressed breath, wishing yet again he'd kept his mouth shut, and wondering what it was about this woman that loosened his usually reticent tongue. But it was too late now to take it back.

"Not when I was so attracted to you myself," he admitted, his voice tight. Her eyes widened, and she drew back slightly, but he kept on. Now that he'd started, he was going to finish. "It just didn't seem fair. Like fighting somebody who couldn't fight back. He was dead, he couldn't compete, couldn't defend himself."

Paige was staring at him. He wondered what she was thinking, what was going on in that agile mind. Then he wondered if maybe he was better off not knowing.

Would he have been better off if he hadn't admitted any of this? But that didn't seem any fairer than bad-mouthing her newly deceased husband.

Paige cut directly to the heart of the matter.

"Then why didn't you come back?" she asked.

He sighed heavily. "Because I felt so damned guilty after that night. When you told me to leave, I figured you would never want to lay eyes on me again."

She lapsed into silence again. She was still watching him. He wanted to look away, to dodge the intensity of her steady gaze. But the fact that she appeared almost stunned kept him right where he was, waiting. Hoping.

Then a loud buzzer sounded, and he knew his chance was gone. For now.

Paige heard the sound of the electronically controlled buzzer announcing the start of school, but for a long moment she didn't—couldn't—move. What Noah had said put an entirely different spin on what he'd done five years ago. And put an entirely different spin on her own actions as well. Had she somehow picked up on some signal, had she really not misinterpreted his intentions at all?

Had he—she barely dared wonder—felt the same heat and power and churning response that she had?

She heard the clatter and chatter of the children coming

in, and that did rouse her out of her stunned state. She got to her feet.

"Mind if I watch?" he asked.

She did mind, because his presence unsettled her. But she could hardly say so, especially now, in front of the kids who were already scrambling into their seats.

"Fine. Have a seat, anywhere you want."

He resumed his place on the sofa, and after a moment of watching the kids come in, spot him and get suddenly quiet, he leaned back and propped his feet up on the table, as if sending a silent signal they should relax. She appreciated his understanding and was pleasantly surprised that he'd picked up on the mood so quickly and done something about it.

The kids still settled down rather more quickly than usual, and she knew it was Noah's presence. The ones whose parents worked for Redstone knew who he was, of course, and she wouldn't be surprised if some of the others did, too. Lani in particular, she thought as she saw the girl sliding Rider sideways glances. She wondered what Kyle had told her.

She introduced him briefly, telling them that he had ten days to do the equivalent of what they had to do in an entire semester. Noah laughed at that and told the kids it wasn't nearly as much fun, though, since he didn't have a smart and pretty teacher to help him go the right way.

Paige tried not to blush. But what he'd said to her was glowing in her mind, seared into her memory. She desperately wanted some time alone to absorb his revelation and decide how she felt about it, but she knew she wasn't going to get that now. Especially not if Noah stayed. As, it seemed, he was content to do.

She went through each grade's assignments for the afternoon, and he seemed perfectly content to loll on the sofa, feet up, watching and listening as if he had absolutely nothing better to do. She knew that wasn't true, not two days before the first high-rolling guests were due to arrive.

When the general announcements were done, she ushered the youngest group, consisting of eleven children ages five to seven, up-front. It was their turn on the computers. The next group was ages eight to twelve, and she set them to work drawing pictures to illustrate the story she'd read to them yesterday. The next group skipped to fourteen and up. That group was Kyle's and Lani's, and she got them set up to work on the debate they were putting together. She'd given them the circumstances of a situation and asked each of them to write it based on how they personally would deal with it. Later they would argue all the points of view they'd come up with. That the circumstances were those of a famous event, she would tell them later, when they compared their results to the actual history.

Rider seemed fascinated by it all, and Paige began to wonder if he was going to spend all afternoon with them. When she had everyone started on their work, she debated whether to join him, but decided she couldn't disrupt her teaching routine because he'd dropped in, and started her usual rounds. She managed to give each group individual attention and made sure to talk to each child alone for at least a few minutes each day; if there were any problems, she wanted to know about them now, not get blindsided later.

When she moved over to the computer center, Noah got up and joined her. "Something I at least know something about," he explained.

"Do you work in that big building we saw?" one of the boys asked.

Noah looked at Paige questioningly. "I showed them Redstone headquarters online," she said.

"Oh. Yes, sometimes. I have an office there."

"Are you way up high?" Hannah, the girl nearest him, asked.

"Sort of. I'm on the twelfth floor."

Her eyes widened, and Paige wondered if he realized that if the girl had spent her entire life here, she well might have never seen a building that tall.

"That's three times as tall as the tallest building here at the resort," he said, and her eyes got even bigger.

And then the questions started coming fast and furious, from all of the kids, but mostly from Hannah. He slid up to sit on one of the tables and for a moment glanced at Paige. She smiled at his expression. He looked as if he knew this was what kept teachers going. Just watching those young minds soak things in, and seeing them coming up with the most unexpected and fascinating questions, was somehow invigorating.

Even if you do look like you've been put in the hot seat, she told him silently.

He glanced at Paige again, and she knew he saw the grin she was trying to keep under wraps. He grinned back, and she thought she saw traces of relief in his eyes, and she wondered if he hadn't been sure until this moment that he was really forgiven.

What happened now—where they would go from here—she had no idea. She had every reason to be wary of a man who traveled as her husband had. She had every reason to—

The crash at the back of the room spun every head around. A man in camouflage leaped into the room. The same man she'd seen in the trees.

Rider slid from the table back to his feet. For a split second he glanced at Paige, almost as if he thought she might know this man.

The smaller door behind her desk burst open, slamming hard against the wall. The clock above it bounced, then crashed to the floor. Another man. In camouflage.

A child somewhere in the back began to scream. Another began to cry.

With reason, Paige thought, as she stared at the two men who had invaded this peaceful place. Both of them were carrying automatic weapons.

Chapter 8

More children were screaming and crying now. Paige moved toward the smallest ones. Rider tensed. One of the men yelled and waved his weapon at her. It looked like the photographs he'd seen of Russian AK-47s, and Rider's mind went immediately to their relative proximity to Cuba. Whatever the weapon was, the sight of it stopped Paige in her tracks.

One of the youngest children, tears streaming down his face, broke and ran toward Paige. The man at the small door swung his weapon around and aimed it at the child.

"Stevie, no!" Paige screamed, and before Rider could stop her she was moving toward the little boy.

For a frozen instant of time, Rider saw it all happening. Saw in his mind a bloody, ugly vision of spraying gunfire and falling children. And Paige. Paige who never thought about what she was risking, only that there was a terrified child who needed her. He knew how one wrong move in a situation like this could bring on disaster and tragedy. But that move had already been made. The only thing he could do was try to keep the aftermath from turning into that bloody vision.

He snapped back to real time. He spun on his heel. He took two steps toward the man aiming at the child.

"Hold your fire!" the older man who had come in the big door shouted.

The younger man stopped. Rider stopped. Paige swept down on the child like a guardian angel. She picked him up and put her body between him and the itchy gunman. The initial threat of a massacre seemed to subside.

The older man—although he still didn't look much over thirty, Rider thought—moved toward the children at the back of the room. He started with the group of the littlest, from which the boy who had come within seconds of dying had broken loose.

"Move! All of you. Up front."

He gestured with one hand rather than the weapon. Rider wondered if that was to lessen the fear that could immobilize the kids, or if he just didn't want the thing to go off by accident.

Rider heard a smothered sob and glanced over to see Hannah, the little girl who had been so wide-eyed and enthused, now fighting tears. He edged back toward her. The itchy one's head snapped around, along with his weapon, and Rider held up his hands. But he kept moving until he was next to the girl. The younger man apparently decided his superior's order still held and lowered the deadly rifle.

Rider reached for Hannah, and she buried her face against him. He put his arm around her, squeezing gently, trying to give her what reassurance he could.

The older man moved toward the next cubicle and did the same as before, herding the kids toward them. Even the oldest ones were clearly terrified. Rider saw a very pale Kyle swipe quickly at his eyes. The lovely girl he'd noticed earlier, however, while obviously frightened, was dry-eyed, watching the armed men with a steady expression.

When all the children were gathered in the front of the schoolroom, the first man jerked his head toward the younger man, who quickly ran back to the door he'd come in. He leaned outside, picked up a duffel bag and set it inside the door, then took up a guarding stance. The older man then took a small, rather battered-looking walkie-talkie from his belt and spoke into it.

"The school is secured."

The radio crackled back something, but from where he was Rider couldn't hear it. Not that he needed to: the presence alone of the radio told him enough for the moment. These men were organized, there were more of them and they were equipped well enough to have radio communication.

They obviously had some kind of objective, Rider thought. Although right at the moment it seemed to be simply terrifying everyone. Successfully, he noted. Everybody in this room—including himself—was afraid.

He watched with jaw clenched as the younger man searched Paige, running his hands over her with thinly disguised glee. Paige stood in stony silence, her face completely still. The older man did a cursory search of Rider, clearly interested only in weapons, however unlikely it might be that there would be any here in the small school. But, as a result, the man missed the cell phone that was virtually invisible in the loose shirt pocket.

"Now," the older man commanded. "You will all stay quiet and behave. No one moves without clearance from me. We will be here until we get what we want, so be smart and don't do anything foolish."

The tension in the room ratcheted up a notch. Some huddled together, some clung to each other, some simply stared in detached shock. But the fear was uppermost in every face.

Every face except one.

He'd meant only to glance at Paige, to make sure she

was holding together, not that he doubted her. But what he saw stopped his gaze dead. He knew the look too well, since it had so recently been directed at him.

Paige Cooper wasn't afraid.

She was furious.

Seated on her sofa, Paige cuddled little Stevie, who had calmed down enough to breathe between sobs. She tried to be gentle, but the anger that was boiling in her made it a difficult task.

She knew who these men were. Oh, not specifically, but the specifics didn't matter, not with soulless brutes like this. No matter what their cause, they were all alike in one critical way: they didn't care who they hurt or killed or how many lives they destroyed in their single-minded fanaticism. She squeezed Stevie tighter. Like the cowards they were, they preyed on the innocent—people who had nothing to do with whatever their ultimate goal was—rather than face their enemy openly. Men like these had murdered her husband, and regardless of their problems, Phil had been the father of her son, and Kyle had been devastated at the loss.

Her anger burned hotter. She had left everything behind to come to this remote place for peace, and now the ugliness had invaded even here.

The older of the two invaders walked over to where Paige was huddled on the sofa with the little boy.

"Keep them all quiet," he ordered her. "I do not like noisy children."

Paige looked up at him, letting every bit of contempt she was feeling show in her face and echo in her voice. "You've already bought your ticket to hell with your actions. Go use it."

The man frowned. She could see him working it out, and by the time he realized exactly what she'd just told him to do, she had turned back to the boy and refused to look at him again.

"I think you fail to realize who is in charge here," he said to her. Paige ignored him. After a moment he said, "No matter. You will know soon enough."

Then he walked away and took up a position at the door he'd come in. His younger counterpart was at the other door. Only then did Paige risk a look around. The children had calmed a bit, what crying there was was mostly silent or at least hushed. She felt a little jolt of pride as she realized the oldest ones, even Kyle, were helping the youngest, hugging them, holding on.

Even Noah was doing his part: Hannah, the girl who'd been asking him questions, was clinging to him like a lifeline. But Paige realized he wasn't looking at Hannah but at her, with an expression of both apprehension and something warmer, almost like admiration.

She didn't know what he could be admiring. She felt on the verge of completely losing control, whether to her own fear or anger she wasn't sure. But she knew neither would do the children any good, so she tried desperately to regain some equilibrium.

She looked over at Kyle again. He had a couple of the smallest children beside him, and on the other side he had Lani. She could tell he was trying to act protectively, but she saw in his face he was as scared as they all were. He looked up then, as if he'd felt her gaze, and in that moment she was looking at the child she remembered. Whatever problems they'd been having weren't between them now.

Kyle opened his mouth to speak. In the instant before he got out "Mom," Noah suddenly coughed, loud enough to draw the boy's attention. Paige saw Noah give a slight, sharp shake of his head. Kyle looked puzzled—no more than she herself felt—but lapsed back into silence.

Noah looked at her then, and caught her frown. His gaze

flicked to the man back at the doors, then to Kyle and back to her, again with that little shake of his head.

Her frown deepened, as did her puzzlement. She didn't know what Noah was trying to communicate. She also wondered why nothing was happening, why the armed men seemed only to be waiting.

Noah leaned over and whispered something to Hannah, who wiped at her eyes and nodded. He patted her on the back, then started to walk toward Paige. Instantly the younger man, the one who seemed to want to shoot first and not bother with questions after, had his weapon trained on Noah.

"I said not to move without permission!" the older one snapped from the main doors.

"Look, it's my back," Noah said, sounding meek and almost whiny. "I can't stand up for too long."

Paige frowned; she'd never noticed him having a problem before. Of course, she hadn't seen him on his feet at length, either, except for the welcome speech he'd given the first day. And given her state of mind when she'd realized it was him, she didn't think she could trust her memories of that. She'd never heard this tone of voice from him, either, but then she'd obviously never seen him in a situation like this.

"Sit, then," the apparent leader said, with an expression that said he had little patience for such minor complaints. He went back to digging into his duffel bag for whatever he'd been after when Noah had moved. God knew what terrorists carted around with them, Paige thought.

Noah walked to the sofa and sat down close to her, but not close enough to draw their captors' attention. He reached out and tweaked Stevie's cheek and gave the child a reassuring smile. Then, still looking down at the boy, he spoke in a low voice clearly meant only for her.

"It's better if they don't know he's yours."

It took her a second, but then she got it. He didn't want

Kyle to betray that he was her son. She thought about that and then realized his point. If they knew he was her son, and if she didn't do exactly what they wanted, they might try to use Kyle to force her to comply. She never would have thought of it herself, but she knew he was right.

She peeked up at Noah, saw he was now looking at her, and she quickly, barely nodded to indicate she understood.

She glanced at the two men. "Why here?" she muttered under her breath, not really expecting an answer.

"Probably because the island's containable," Noah said, still keeping his voice low. "And there's just the staff here now, with no real security yet. They won't be coming in until the guests do. And as long as they hold the children, the parents will cooperate."

His calm assessment, at odds with the near whine she'd heard moments ago, surprised her.

"But what could they want here?" she asked.

He shrugged. "Maybe it's just about Redstone. Josh is always a target for any disgruntled group who wants to strike out at wealth or power. They don't care that he came up the hard way, from a worse start than most of them ever had."

"In my experience," Paige said tightly, "they don't care about anyone."

Still, she was surprised at his astute assessment. She supposed he had to know about such things, the way he gallivanted around the world. But that he was calm enough to think about it when they were almost literally looking down the barrel of a gun was unexpected.

For a long time nothing happened. They all just sat still. The children were afraid to move, and Paige was growing angrier by the moment. Terrorizing children was beyond cowardice, it was evil. This was the second time in her life she'd confronted this kind of malignancy, and she found it even more repugnant now than she had before. No matter what they were after, no matter what injustice they felt had been done them, nothing justified this. Nothing.

"I wonder what they're waiting for," Noah said softly, his voice so quiet she doubted anybody more than two feet away could have heard him.

Paige felt something jump then tighten inside her. Yes, she'd wondered why nothing was happening, but somehow Noah's phrasing, that they were waiting for something specific, made the lack of activity now even more ominous. She hadn't thought they might be simply waiting for something, some sign or order. and she didn't want to think of what the result of that sign or order might be.

She looked at the younger man, the one who made her most nervous because of his apparent desire to shoot when anything at all happened. He was lounging against the doorjamb behind her desk, the powerful, threatening-looking rifle cradled in his arms like a baby. She wondered what sort of twisted mind could come so close to murdering a child, yet would take such loving care of a lethal weapon. She believed guns had their place, but that place was most certainly not in the hands of a man who apparently saw nothing wrong with that dichotomy.

The older man at the main doors, however, seemed much more restless. She didn't know if his constant glances outside were merely wariness, watchfulness or if he was actually expecting something. And if he was expecting something, she wondered what.

Maybe, she thought, they were afraid someone would be coming to rescue them. That idea cheered her until she realized the catastrophe it could turn into, with the children caught in the middle.

She looked over at Kyle. He was sitting with his arm around Lani, who for once wasn't lecturing him on his attitude. Kyle was clearly trying to comfort her, and she was proud of him for that. Her son, the boy she remembered, the generous, smiling boy who had loved her, was still in there somewhere. And she would reach him. Somehow. She would—

The sudden movement of the older man stopped her thoughts. He leaned partially out the door, as if peering at something in the distance. Then he came back and shouted urgently to his companion.

"Filipo! He is coming!"

The younger man, the swaggering, trigger-happy one, snapped to attention. He stood up straight, rifle at the ready. His expression, which had until now consisted of an arrogance-tinged smirk, became impassive, even stern.

Paige glanced at Noah. He lifted a brow and his mouth twisted at one corner, indicating he, too, realized that this was what they'd been waiting for. Whoever the "he" was, he was obviously the leader of these two, and possibly this entire operation. Whatever this operation was.

She had a feeling they were about to find out.

She heard the footsteps on the stairs, then a heavy, measured tread across the small porch. This was followed by other footsteps, more than one set, she thought.

She realized she was holding her breath, but couldn't seem to make herself let it out. A man stepped inside. He was wearing regular green fatigues, not camouflage. He carried no rifle, but had a sidearm in a covered holster at his hip. She had a chance to study him as he paused to speak to the man at the doors.

He was taller than both of the men who had taken over the school but not quite as tall as Noah. He was older than both, as well, judging by the faint touch of silver at the temples in his otherwise brown hair. Although, not much older, perhaps mid to late thirties, with clean-cut, pleasant features.

Apparently finished with their discussion, the newcomer looked over his shoulder toward the outside and made a summoning gesture. Two other men, near duplicates of the first two, down to the rifles and camouflage, stepped into the schoolroom. They took up positions, one in front and one behind the man who was clearly a leader of some sort. Then the entourage of three headed toward the front of the schoolroom.

The children stirred restlessly, made nervous all over again by this new threat.

"Shhh," Paige said, trying to soothe them.

The two escorts split and went to each side of the area where the children were sitting. The leader came toward the sofa. He glanced at Noah assessingly. Noah seemed to sink down into the cushions, as if trying to disappear, and after a moment the man shifted his gaze to Paige.

He waited, as if expecting her to rise to her feet. *Not likely,* she told him silently.

She couldn't help noticing he had ridiculously long and thick eyelashes. In fact, if you set aside who he was and what he was doing, he might be considered a rather handsome man...if you also set aside the unnatural brightness in his eyes that made Paige think of drugs or madness.

Paige knew she could never set any of that aside, knew that to her he could only be ugly.

And after a moment he seemed to think better of waiting for her to rise and spoke.

"You are Mrs. Cooper? I am called Ares."

His English was slightly accented, but rather formal. That he knew her name bothered her. "I wondered what silly name you would pick to make yourself feel like a man," she muttered.

A pair of dark, almost femininely arched eyebrows shot upward in surprise. She knew he'd heard her, but he apparently decided to pretend he hadn't.

"I am the leader of the People's Freedom Cell of Arethusa."

She glanced at the two escorts. "Such a brave leader that you must have four armed men with you to face a room of schoolchildren?"

The man called Ares tensed.

"Paige, stop," Noah urged. "Don't antagonize him."

"And who are you?" Ares asked, frowning at Noah.

"Me? I'm just a fellow teacher."

Ares didn't look convinced.

"He's a supervisor," Paige said quickly, much more calmly. "He's here to monitor my class."

Unimpressed, Ares turned back to her. "In any case, he is right. Do not antagonize me."

As quickly as that her calm deserted her again. "I've lived through the worst your kind can do. You don't scare me."

To her surprise the man laughed suddenly. "I was told you were a special woman. I can see that is correct."

He spoke it as a compliment, but the laughing words stabbed fear through Paige like a bayonet. *He was told?*

All of a sudden this went from a random, impossible-to-understand bit of terrorist insanity to something much more personal. Something, at least in some way, aimed at her. She fought to regain some semblance of composure, knowing she didn't dare lose it now, not when the children were in jeopardy.

"First," Ares said, with every evidence of cheer, "let me warn you not to expect any help. My men hold the entire premises, and have secured everyone on the hotel grounds. We also control all communications apparatus. No call can be made without our knowledge. There will be no rescue."

Paige looked quickly at the children, but either the man's words hadn't gotten through their shock or they didn't realize he'd just told many of them their parents were now also hostages. She hoped it stayed that way; they were already scared enough without adding fear for their parents into the mix.

With a suppressed shiver she looked back at their captor.

"I have heard," the man said, "that you are a fair

woman. That you teach your students to see both sides of a situation."

She wanted to look away, but the man called Ares never took his eyes off her, and she wouldn't let herself look away until he did, no matter how frightened she was by the fact that someone had apparently talked to this man about her.

"That makes you a lucky woman," Ares told her. "You will be moved to the hotel. Your things will be brought to you, and you will be treated well."

"I can't leave these children!" The words burst from her.

"My men will stay with them."

"That does *not* make me feel any better," she said, her tone sarcastic as her fear ebbed a little in the face of his absurd effort at reassuring her.

"Then your superior can stay, as well," he said, jerking a thumb at Noah, "if you like."

"And who do I have to betray for these thirty pieces of silver?"

"Betray?" Was he mocking her with that tone of utter innocence? "Why, no one. In fact, the opposite. You will be in a position to save many lives."

With a great effort Paige hid the shiver that rippled through her at his indirect admission that lives might be lost before this was over. In an inane flash she remembered her journal entry, and suddenly knew exactly how the woman in that book had felt, as if she'd brought all this down upon herself with her silly musings.

"You will be," Ares said grandly, "the spokesperson."

Her fear faded, replaced by bewilderment. "Spokesperson? For whom?"

"Why, the hostages, of course."

Her breath caught. She glanced toward the children, toward Kyle, but Ares shook his head. "Not them," he said impatiently. "They are merely insurance. I'm speaking of the true hostages. The ones to come, who can get the attention of the world.''

She heard Noah suck in a breath. And it hit her then: Ares was talking about the wealthy, high-profile guests who would be arriving in two days.

''Ah, I see you understand. Very good. So you comprehend the honor I have given you.''

''Honor?'' Her voice was tight.

''Indeed. You will become a celebrity of sorts, when the media arrive.''

She blinked. ''The media?''

''Of course. As soon as everything is secure, they will be notified of our takeover. And you will be the voice of the hostages. You are a woman, a teacher, the world will believe you. You will tell the world they are being treated well, that we are reasonable men and that we should be given what we ask for.''

Paige did rise then. She stood because she could no longer sit still in the face of this insanity.

''People held against their will have no voice,'' she said icily, matching his formality of speech. ''Nor do reasonable men do such abhorrent things. I truly hope that you are given *exactly* what you are asking for.''

Her words slowed him for a moment, but she saw the anger flash in his eyes when he understood what she had meant.

She barely saw his hand move. In the next instant pain slammed through her head as he backhanded her on the side of the head. She heard Kyle yell ''No!'' heard someone else swear, realized it was Noah only when he leaped to his feet. She fell back on the sofa, her ears ringing, tears welling up, tears she would *not* let Ares see. And despite the pain she felt a sense of triumph that enabled her to fight back the tears before they spilled over. She'd gotten to him. She'd stuck him right in his ego.

''Sit down!'' Ares ordered Noah.

Do it, Paige pled silently.

"Go to hell," Noah spat out. "And if you touch her again I'll send you there myself."

Paige, startled by his fervent defense, looked up just in time to see Ares make the slightest of motions with one finger toward the trigger-happy guard. The man gleefully raised his rifle, aimed it toward Noah and fired.

Chapter 9

Paige knew she'd let out a little scream at the shot, but it was nothing compared to the wailing that now arose from several of the children. If she hadn't been looking right at Noah, if she couldn't see that he was still standing, unhurt, she'd have done worse than scream.

Slowly Noah turned his head. She saw where he was looking, saw the hole that had appeared in the wall of the room, directly behind where he was standing. Grimacing, Noah sank slowly back down onto the sofa. The sound of the children's sobbing ebbed slightly, as again the older students hushed them.

"The next time," Ares warned, "I will not tell him to miss."

Noah stared at his knees and swallowed visibly.

"And you," Ares said, glaring down at Paige, "you will stay here, along with these children, until you change your mind. And you *will* change your mind. Or you will pay dearly, I promise you that."

He looked up and called orders to the first two men, the

ones who had taken over the school. "Tarak, Filipo, you will guard both doors of the building. Be watchful and careful. I want no one hurt. Yet. I'm trusting you."

Paige barely heard; his words were echoing in her head. *Pay dearly.*

Paige surreptitiously peeked at Noah from the corner of her eye, grateful that he had had the foresight to see that keeping Kyle's relationship to her a secret would be wise. He didn't seem to notice her glance. Now he was staring at his hands, which were knotted in his lap.

As Ares snapped at his two escorts to follow him and strode angrily out of the school, something else occurred to her. Instead of striking her across the face, as she might have expected, the man had instead hit the side of her head. She'd thought he was just striking out wildly, but what if it had been intentional? What if he'd hit her where he could be sure it wouldn't show when he was trying to convince the world his captives were being treated well?

Somehow, the idea that he could think so clearly, never losing sight of his plan even in anger, chilled her more than a bout of uncontrolled rage would have.

When they were again alone with the original two men, Paige risked looking at Noah. He hadn't moved. In fact, he seemed utterly, totally chastened by his near-fatal encounter with the man.

She couldn't blame him for being rattled, not after coming that close to death. And he'd done it for her, after all, leaping to her defense after Ares had struck her, so she should give him a lot of credit for that. Still, she was surprised he'd so completely collapsed. It was such a change from the dynamic, take-charge man she'd always seen.

But then, he'd probably never been shot at before, either, she admitted. It probably wasn't a common risk in his job. In fact, ironically and sadly, it was probably less of a risk for him than it was for most teachers these days. And he had stood up in the face of five armed men when Ares had hit her.

She'd be doing the same thing, in his place. In fact, she felt like doing it right now, just sitting down and giving in to the tremors that were so hard to quell. But she couldn't. She had a roomful of kids counting on her.

She glanced at Noah once more and then turned back to the children.

Rider watched the two guards as best he could without betraying himself, his mind racing. In the wake of their leader's visit, they acted as if they'd been honored by what was clearly simple guard duty. If this was a sign of Ares's power over his troops, they were dealing with the worst kind of charisma-blinded zealots.

They both seemed quite enamored of their roles. And now he had to choose what his role was going to be. The closest he'd ever come to actual combat was reading Sun-Tzu. And while the millennia-old treatise on the art of war was concise and educational, he'd been reading it as a businessman, not a warrior. Had the situation not been so grim, he would have laughed aloud at the idea of himself as a warrior of any kind. He'd never even been in the service. What could he possibly do?

But somebody had to do something—that was clear. And he was, theoretically, the person in charge while he was here. There was no way around it, it was up to him.

Still, the circumstances limited him greatly. Surprise and his wits were the only weapons he had, and he could only think of one possibility of how to best use them. It was a twisted path, but hadn't Sun-Tzu said that he who perceives the circuitous route as direct would be victorious? Something like that, anyway.

It wasn't going to be easy. Paige was already looking at him in an odd way, with a touch of near disappointment. Even the guards were looking at him with scorn. And it would only get worse if this worked. He'd just have to live with that. He sat silently, thinking, turning over options, until he had a loose sort of a plan. He didn't like it, but he couldn't think of anything better. And he couldn't just sit here and wait.

Still, because he knew what her reaction would be, it took him a moment to work up to looking at Paige as she comforted the children and saying, loudly enough for the hothead at the closest door to hear, "Maybe you should reconsider."

She turned and stared at him, dumfounded, and it was worse than he'd expected. "What?"

"Maybe you should work with them. It might make it easier on all of us."

"You want me to become a mouthpiece for this…this scum?" she exclaimed.

That did it, he thought, seeing both the guards suddenly start paying attention.

"It's better than getting beaten up and shot at," he said, coming as close as he thought he could to a whine without going over the top.

The look in her eyes went from shocked to bewildered to, he was very much afraid, disgust. "You'd really have me cooperate with them? They're a disease on the planet, and you want me to *help* them?"

Damn, he was proud of her! He wanted to kiss her, but he schooled his voice to a wheedling tone now. "What can it hurt? They can't want anything very important. Probably only money, that's all their kind care about, really."

"Shut up!" shouted the hotheaded Filipo. "You know nothing!"

Bingo, thought Rider. He was about to open his mouth when Paige spoke, following his lead as perfectly as if she had a script before her.

"I suppose," she said to Filipo, in a voice that chilled even Rider, "you're going to tell me you have some kind of noble cause, that you're above such things as hostage taking for mere money."

She'd played into his plans perfectly, but Noah still wished she would take it a little easier. Although, perhaps she'd realized that when Ares had said he wanted no one hurt—yet—he'd particularly meant her. Still, she wasn't doing herself any favors by provoking these two.

"We fight injustice!" Filipo cried. "We fight for the release of our brothers, rotting in an Arethusan prison. Money means nothing to us."

"Especially," Rider said almost conversationally to Paige, "since they probably have no shortage of it. Most terrorist groups in this region are also drug smugglers."

Filipo swore and took a step toward them. Only a shout from Tarak across the room stopped him. "Do not let them play you like a flute," he warned.

"Take it easy," Noah put in, holding up his hands in meek surrender. "I'm sorry, I was just mouthing off."

Filipo fell back, grumbling. But he resumed his post at the door.

He probably should have kept his mouth shut, Rider thought. But the outraged loftiness of the man had grated. He knew from the in-depth studies Redstone had done before starting the resort that what he'd said was accurate. And coupled with his quick, sniveling backpedaling, it might just make what he had to do more believable. He had only to look at Paige's face to see that he'd been convincing.

The sickened feeling he had when he saw her looking at him with such hurt bewilderment was trying to tell him something, but he didn't have time to sort it out now. Now he had to concentrate on the job at hand. Whether he liked it or not.

To Paige the afternoon seemed endless. The only thing that seemed to happen was that about every half hour, one of their two guards—they seemed to trade off—would close his door and walk away, apparently to check the area surrounding the school. After these regular patrols they would return and take up their posts again.

Despite their initial fear, the younger children soon became restless. And the more restless they became, the edgier Tarak, the older guard, became. He had apparently been telling the truth when he'd said he didn't like noisy children. And when she had reluctantly been allowed to escort a couple of the younger ones to the bathroom in the back, off the vestibule, things had only gotten worse while she was out of sight.

Finally Tarak left his post and strode down the center aisle, treading heedlessly down the barefoot paths, until he stopped in front of Paige.

"Make them be quiet," he ordered her.

"They're children," she retorted sharply. "They're children and you've frightened them. They should have gone home long ago, and you're making them stay here, away from their parents. What do you expect?"

"I expect them to be quiet! And if you do not make them, I will tie them all up and tape their mouths shut!"

That threat got through to several of the children, and the noise level grew instantly, wails joining with children scrambling to cling to Paige.

"Well, that helped a lot," Paige told the man sourly.

Tarak glared at her. "You are far too disrespectful, for a woman. When this is over and we have gotten what we wanted, I will let Filipo teach you not to be."

"When this is over, you'll have no one to teach but your cell mate," Paige returned.

Rider winced inwardly, yet at the same time he wanted to cheer her. Tarak opened his mouth, then shut it again. Was he seeing the futility of carrying on a battle of wits when he was unarmed and his opponent had a howitzer? Rider thought with a grin he had to stifle.

"Just keep them quiet," Tarak ordered, and stalked back to his post.

"And just how," Paige muttered, "am I supposed to do that?"

How was she supposed to keep restless kids quiet? Rider had no answer. She was the teacher, not him. The only thing he knew about it was old memories of his own school days, longer ago than he cared to remember. Back then, the only thing—

He looked at Paige. "Read to them."

She blinked. "What?"

"Read to them. Isn't that what teachers do for quiet times?"

She waved a hand toward the gathered kids. "I've got twenty-six kids here, of all ages. What on earth am I going to read that will keep them all quiet? There's not a book around that..."

Her voice trailed off. He could almost see her thinking. She turned to look at the kids, specifically at the girl Rider had seen Kyle mooning after.

"Lani? Do you still have the book I gave you? The wizard book?"

The girl looked up, startled. "Yes, I do."

"May I borrow it back for a while?"

The girl nodded. "Of course. But it's in my bag. In the back."

Paige stood up. Without a glance at the guard behind them she started walking toward the main doors. Tarak shifted his weapon. Paige kept going.

The woman wasn't afraid of anything, Rider thought. And he wondered how much of that quiet courage she'd found since Phil's desertion and death.

"What are you doing?" Tarak asked sharply as she came up to him.

"If you want them to be quiet, then you'd better let me do this."

After a moment he let her pass, but he kept his eyes and his rifle trained on her as she disappeared into the vestibule. Rider held his breath. Less than two minutes later she was back in the doorway, a thick hardcover book in her hands. Tarak looked at it as if to inspect it. Rider saw Paige say something, saw the guard glare at her yet again, then waved her on with an annoyed gesture.

She'd probably made some crack about smuggling a weapon in the book, Rider thought, wondering if she would ever be able to pass up a chance to needle their captors. Then again, as long as they were under a mandate not to hurt her, she could do the rest of them nothing but good by keeping the men focused on her, while he sat back meekly cowering.

When she returned to the front of the room, she pulled up a seat he hadn't noticed before, a director's-style folding chair the height of a bar stool. She settled into it, the book on her lap. By then most of the kids were watching her.

"If we're going to be stuck here awhile," Paige told them, "we might as well escape in a different way." She opened the book to the first page and began the story of a young boy about to learn he was a wizard.

It took a while, but after a few pages the kids had settled down and were listening. Even the older ones, Rider noted. He couldn't blame them, not only was the story engrossing, but Paige read it well, like a storyteller herself. Once he even thought he caught Filipo tuning in, although he turned away quickly when he realized Rider had seen him.

Paige read and read, until her voice started to sound scratchy. Rider found himself getting as wrapped up in the story of the mistreated young boy who discovered he was a wizard as the kids were. But he also noticed the time passing, and wondered what Tarak and Filipo were going to do when they had a bunch of hungry, tired kids on their hands.

As if she'd had the same thought at the same moment,

when she reached the end of the next chapter, Paige looked up from the pages. "You're going to have to feed these children," she told Tarak in an almost belligerent tone that told Rider she'd fight if she had to.

"Food will come," Tarak said shortly.

She went back to her reading until the light began to fade. Then she slid off the chair and started toward the wall. Filipo moved immediately to stop her.

"I need light to continue," she explained.

"No lights," Tarak said from the back.

She turned to him. "No lights? You want tired, hungry children to stay quiet in the dark?"

"They will not be hungry. The food is on the way. And they will be quiet, because they will be sleeping."

Rider thought the man was being a bit optimistic. He himself might not know much about kids, but he didn't think any of them over the age of ten were real keen on going to sleep the instant it was dark. But he understood the no-lights order: it was like going hunting and, when it got dark, staring into the fire. You destroyed your night vision, and by the time you got it back, you could be dead. Besides, the moon was nearly full and cast more light than most people realized, at least for eyes adjusted to the night.

The man had told the truth about the food. The sound of footsteps came shortly after his words, accompanied by the clatter of dishes. Two more armed men came in, loaded down with food on banquet-style, covered plates stacked on huge trays. Different men than before, a lower rung than the bodyguards, Rider guessed. Elected for this detail because Ares wouldn't allow any of the hotel personnel outside, especially not to see their children.

The men set the trays down on Paige's desk while making a couple of jokes about baby-sitting that made Filipo bristle and Tarak retort unkindly about their respective mothers. Laughing, the food carriers left.

"You will each get a fork, nothing else," Tarak instructed. "And they will all be accounted for when you are done, or no one will eat the next time. You have one half hour."

The two guards retreated to eat their own meal, although they took turns so one was always watching. Paige ignored her own food and set about coaxing the younger ones, upset all over again at the sight of yet more armed men, to eat. The guards seemed to regard this as unthreatening and didn't challenge her. Rider gulped down what he could of the meal he barely tasted, knowing he was going to need the fuel. Then he went to Paige.

"Go eat. I'll do this now."

"I don't know," she began.

Unsure what else to do, Rider appealed to the little ones. "You don't mind, do you? If I sit with you, so Mrs. Cooper can eat? She's hungry, too."

The kids looked doubtfully at him, but their regard for Paige won out, as he'd hoped. She still hesitated, but when he insisted, she did as he asked and sat down at her desk to hastily eat, all the while watching the children. Redstone Resorts had a reputation for fine cuisine, but Rider somehow doubted whether he or Paige could tell anybody what they'd just eaten.

By the time the half hour was up and their guards began to collect and count the forks, it was past twilight and growing dark. "Get them ready to sleep," Tarak instructed.

Paige laughed in his face. Tarak tensed. Rider winced yet again. "You don't have kids, do you?" she asked the man.

"I do," Tarak retorted. "But *my* children are properly obedient!"

"And terrified of their father?"

"Respectful," Tarak said. "Now do it!"

Rider feared he was losing patience with his troublesome hostage.

"Why does he always yell at her?" little Hannah asked him as he knelt beside her chair.

"She's angry about what he's doing, keeping you all here," Rider explained, "so he gets angry back."

"I don't like it," Hannah said firmly.

"I don't, either," Rider told her. "So we've got to do what she wants us to, so she's not so angry, okay?"

He gave her a squeeze and got to his feet. When Paige rejoined him, he pitched his voice low to speak to her.

"You've got to back off, Paige. You might push him too far and somebody could get hurt."

"Including you?" she snapped, although no louder than he had spoken; she might be angry, but she was still thinking. And he'd had that coming, from her point of view.

"Including me, you and the children. Give it a rest, at least for a while. Let's get them settled. It's going to be a long night."

She said nothing more, but began to do as he said. She had a couple of the older kids go to the little ones' cubicle—warily watching Tarak every step of the way—to gather up the mats that were there. They brought them back and then moved the chairs out of the way and laid them out. There were extras, but not enough for all the older kids. Kyle took it upon himself to volunteer the boys to rough it. Lani quickly vetoed that idea.

"Girls can be just as tough as boys," she said firmly.

"Tougher," Kyle said easily. "You have to have the babies."

Rider smothered a grin but gave Kyle an approving wink. Kyle in turn gave him a sideways look that Rider couldn't quite read, although it clearly meant something.

Paige then began the lengthy process of taking the little ones to the bathroom. The older ones she merely escorted, so they wouldn't have to go past the guard alone. Once that was done, and she had the littlest ones settled on the mats, the older ones at least sitting on the floor, Rider casually moved toward her, putting himself between her and Filipo so that he could turn his back to the young guard.

"Let's move the sofa up here," he said, loud enough for both guards to hear, gesturing toward the raised computer center. "If we put it up there on the platform then you can see everyone and anybody who might need something."

For a moment she looked puzzled; there wasn't really anything to be gained by moving it, she could see everybody anyway and he knew she knew that. But when he mouthed "Say yes," at her, after a moment she just nodded.

"All right," she said, loud enough for the guard to hear.

It took them a couple of minutes to lever the sofa up onto the computer platform and get it exactly where he wanted it. Paige clearly didn't understand why it needed to be exactly there, and there was barely room for it, but she helped him, anyway. So, he thought, there was at least some small amount of trust left.

Or she was just withholding final judgment, waiting a bit longer before she wrote him off entirely.

By the time they were done with everything, it was completely dark, although not as dark as it could have been, thanks to the moon. Paige went from child to child, reassuring them with encouraging words that Rider wasn't sure she believed herself. But they seemed to believe her and began to settle down for a night she'd told them to think of as camping out. And if she lingered a tiny bit longer with Kyle, Rider didn't think anyone had noticed. Finally she retreated to the sofa they'd moved, and sank down onto it wearily.

Their two guards had taken chairs to their respective doors and appeared to be settling in for the night, their attention divided between their prisoners and the outside, and broken only by their regular rounds. Time spun out. When at last he was certain neither of them was looking, he walked to the back of the sofa to once more make sure

it was in the right place. Then he went to stand behind
Paige, leaned over and put his hands on her shoulders. He
felt how incredibly tight her muscles were, just before she
instinctively tensed. He rubbed gently and leaned over far-
ther.

"It's going to be okay," he told her. "I promise."

He doubted that she believed him. He didn't blame her
at all, since he had no idea himself if he'd be able to keep
that promise.

Chapter 10

She didn't understand. The terrorists, with their scare tactics, disgusting methods and pseudo-noble demands, seemed downright simple to understand next to Noah Rider. One minute he was acting afraid of his own shadow, next he was calming the kids. He'd been so good with them, even though he insisted he knew next to nothing about dealing with children. And now he was rubbing the tenseness out of her shoulders and telling her it was going to be okay in a voice she almost believed.

Barely aware of what she was doing, she leaned back into his hands, only realizing how knotted her muscles were by the feel of strong yet gentle fingers working them, easing them. She closed her eyes. Just for a minute, she thought. Just for a minute she could stop thinking and just feel the warmth spreading beneath his hands. Just for a minute, and then she'd get back to worrying about their situation.

She felt him move and opened her eyes. She realized he was now kneeling behind the sofa. She started to turn her

head, but stopped when he whispered, "There's nothing
more you can do right now."

She nearly shivered at the feel of his breath against her
ear. And then his fingers brushed the skin at the back of
her neck and she did shiver. How could he do this to her
with just a touch, and in the middle of chaos?

She made herself concentrate on his words. "I can't just
sit here," she said, speaking as quietly as he had, hoping
that in the darkness nothing would draw the guard's attention.

"That's all you can do for now. You have the kids to
think about. If anything happened to you, think what it
would do to them. Look how upset they got when that
bastard hit you."

And you almost got shot, she thought, shivering anew at
the memory. She didn't flinch at all at his epithet. It fit in
most senses of the word.

But he had a point. She hadn't thought of that. She knew
the kids liked her, as well as they could like any teacher
they'd only been with a few weeks. And the little ones
especially had taken to her. And it would be the little ones
who would be affected most if something happened to her.

"Just wait until morning. Things may change by then."

"You mean they may go away? Get what they want and
leave?"

Noah sighed. "Not likely. Not if they want somebody
out of jail in Arethusa. The government won't negotiate.
I've worked with them when we were making the deal for
Redstone Bay, and they're pretty hard-nosed."

"What could change, then?"

"Maybe Ares will have other things to think about besides a spokesperson and leave you alone for the moment."

"Like how to terrorize everyone into being too afraid to
resist?" It was all she could do to maintain a whisper.

"That is the usual MO, I believe," Noah agreed.

How could he sound so cool, almost casual, when she